BE HAPPY

I gather Daddy Dean has something special to talk about today.

"What do you want to be?" he asks.

I think I know the answer to that question. I want to be cuter and smarter. I want to have it all, to be a school leader. I want to be liked by everybody. I want to be somebody else. I know these are not the things Daddy Dean wants to hear. "I want to be happy," I say.

He shakes his head. "No, I mean, what do you want to *do*? When you're . . . older."

"I haven't really thought about it," I say.

He closes his eyes. I sit beside him and wonder what in the world he wants me to do.

Then he opens his eyes. "You're right," he says, out of the blue.

"About what?"

He chuckles. "Be happy," he says.

A
Small
Pleasure

C.B. Christiansen

AN AVON  FLARE BOOK

Thanks to the Pacific Northwest Writers Conference for introducing me to my editor.

AVON BOOKS
A division of
The Hearst Corporation
105 Madison Avenue
New York, New York 10016

First Avon Flare Printing: July 1989

For my father
To my family
To Roger, who listens

A Small Pleasure

Chapter 1

Nature doesn't care about the big plans of a small town girl like me.

This thought occurs to me as Daddy Dean raises his hammer and brings it down—bam, bam, bam—square on the nailhead every time. My hammer is lighter than my father's. My method is hit and miss. Together we pound out a pleasant rhythm. Bam! Tappa-tappa. Bam! Bam! Tap.

Mama insists on dragging out the camera. "Smahl," she orders. We smile, as much at her fading Carolina accent as at her command. Twenty-five years in eastern Washington and she still twangs. She clicks a picture of us on our brand new patio deck.

Then Daddy Dean reaches out to clamp a thick hand on my shoulder. "Good job," he says.

My mouth stretches into a dumb grin. I almost forgot how good it feels to work a project with Daddy Dean. I haven't had time lately, what with my majorette practice, my job at Foamy's drive-in and my three-year plan.

People with plans have to make sacrifices. I read that somewhere. I believe it. I press my

1

hands to the center of my back where a tightness has been growing all this long July afternoon.

"It's that bending," Mama says, "and lifting, too."

I hear the frown in her voice. I know what she is thinking, sitting there in her turquoise-blue, plastic weave lawn chair. She won't come right out and say so, but she is thinking it's wrong for a sixteen-year-old girl to be carting planks of wood on her shoulders. "Take it easy," she tells me again and again.

A girl with ambitions can't take it easy. But Mama wouldn't understand that.

I don't mind the pain. We've worked extra hard to finish the patio by today, Independence Day. If it doesn't rain, Daddy Dean will invite the neighbors for beer and sparklers. If it doesn't rain, I'll perform at the stadium tonight, during the fireworks show.

I try to ignore the sense of gathering that comes before a thunderstorm.

Daddy Dean yawns, big and loud. "How about some iced tea?" He watches Mama head for the house and stretches after the screen door slams behind her. "Smells like rain," he murmurs.

He's right. I hear the rustling of the weeping willow branches. A breeze is up and it does smell like rain. Two weeks of dry weather and nature picks today to make up for it. If it doesn't rain, I'll twirl my fire baton at the stadium. They'll announce my name over the loudspeaker: *Wray. Jean. Child, -ild, -ild.*

When Mama backs out the door with her tray, I see she's brought along a fresh pack of cigarettes. I predict trouble as she hands us our glasses.

The iced tea feels cool going down. It's a nice change from soda. After three years of working at Foamy's drive-in, I've had my fill of root beer.

Mama stirs her tea, twirling up a sugar twister. "Bud and Arlene give you the night off, Wray Jean?"

"No, Poe is working my shift."

"Paulette ought to take it easy," Mama says of my best friend. "She's going to wear herself out."

I don't bother to tell Mama that Poe likes working at Foamy's, that sitting around waiting for life to happen would wear her out more.

I take another big swallow and watch Daddy Dean do the same.

He drains his glass. "Great!" he says.

Mama blushes to the roots of her dust brown hair. She wears the same silly-proud grin I wear when Daddy Dean passes me a compliment. There's no trick to seeing how pleased she is. She automatically reaches for her cigarettes.

Trouble, I think again. The cellophane crackles like a haystack in a flash fire.

Daddy Dean used to gallantly extend a match whenever Mama pulled out a cigarette. "You have the manners of a southern gentleman," she would say, by way of thanking him.

Today he concentrates on fishing an ice cube from his glass. He pretends he doesn't notice Mama waiting.

"Fine!" she finally snaps. "I'll light it myself!"

Daddy Dean slowly rubs the ice over the back

3

of his neck. He stopped lighting Mama's cigarettes last spring, the day they discovered his cancer. "Could have been lung cancer," he said. "But it wasn't," Mama argued. She chain-smoked the whole four hours of his surgery. When Dr. Peck informed us they "got it all," she was so relieved she smoked another half-pack before Daddy Dean came to. I had to send my lucky sweater to Deeker's Dry Cleaners, it smelled so bad of burned tobacco after that.

Now Daddy Dean groans like he does every time Mama opens a new package. "You've gotta quit, Mae," he says. "I did."

"Don't start on me," Mama threatens. She guards her smoking close as a dog with a butcher bone.

"Daddy Dean says it's going to rain," I announce, hoping to change the subject.

But Mama is already mad. "Your father isn't *always* right, Wray Jean." She turns a glare on him. "Why would you tell her a thing like that?"

She pokes her cigarette at the sky. The smoke trail is lost against the clouds. But I don't think Mama sees the clouds at all. She is pointing to a small bright spot, a tiny patch of powder blue.

"See there?" she demands. "Blue sky. No rain. Shame on you for upsetting your daughter."

I bite my lip, wishing I had kept my mouth shut. Daddy Dean winks at me. He seems untouched by Mama's grouching.

"It's not going to rain," she continues. "You'll be the shining star of the whole fireworks show." She flicks an ash off her bermuda shorts and adds shyly, "You look so pretty in your new uniform."

I stare at the bent nails lying by my hand. Daddy Dean's compliments go straight to my heart, but Mama's linger in the air between us, making us both uncomfortable. Besides, I'll be wearing an old costume tonight, a gold-sequined leotard, safe for fire batons. The new uniform is for parades and group routines coming up in the fall.

"The skirt needs hemming," I mumble. "Mine is longer than all the others."

"Oh, why should you care about everyone else," Mama asks. "You worry way too much, Wray Jean. You remind me of your uncle when he was your age."

I picture the big old house in Raleigh, North Carolina, where Uncle Raymond lives with twelve other "boarders" and a couple of social workers. "Crazy Uncle Raymond," I say affectionately. "Crazy like a fox," is what I mean.

"No," Mama says softly, "not crazy. Disappointed." She doesn't have a sense of humor about this. I don't know why. Uncle Raymond is eccentric, that's all.

But I can't help remarking, "Mama, they don't call it Hearthaven Home for the Disappointed."

"They should." She sighs. "He wasn't always that way, you know."

I know. I sigh, too. She's been comparing me to her brother since I can remember, since before he went funny last fall. She never compares Kayla to Uncle Raymond. Of course, my sister is five years older and has always been wiser. Wise enough to earn a 4.0 at the university. Wise enough to land a summer internship this year.

Kayla takes after Mama the way I take after Daddy Dean. She has what Mama calls "common sense."

My sister loves Uncle Raymond because he's a relative. I love him for his attitude: nothing ventured, nothing gained. Only in his case, it turned out to be everything ventured, nothing gained. No wonder he's depressed. He's staying in a small third-story room at Hearthaven while he tries to put his life back together. It won't take forever. Mama is the one who worries too much. I don't see what the length of my majorette skirt has to do with Uncle Raymond's problem.

"I'm not crazy *or* disappointed," I point out. "I'm simply conscientious."

The words sound pompous. I giggle at myself.

Mama shakes her head as if to clear it of such a curiosity as me. "Everything is going to be just fine tonight," she says. "Trust me."

Oh, I want to. I want her to convince me with her downpour of encouraging words.

Daddy Dean picks up his hammer, testing its heft. "Rusty Hayes going to be there?"

His gruff question rattles me. Rusty has been my boyfriend for months, but Daddy Dean hasn't taken to him yet. I shrug. "He's working the Blaine land during pea harvest," I say. "He might make it in. He might not."

Daddy Dean shoots me a quick squint like he's speed-reading my mind. My indifference seems to satisfy him. The truth is, Rusty will be there all right. If it doesn't rain.

"How about the other twirling girlies?" Daddy Dean throws his hammer up. He catches it mid-spin. He loves to pretend it's a joke, my being a baton twirler and all.

"You shouldn't make fun," Mama says. "Wray Jean was selected head majorette because of her leadership qualities."

Leadership qualities. I love the sound of those words. Wilma High is a big school for a small town because all the farm communities feed into it. That makes it hard for a person to stand out. But the head majorette stands out, right in front of the forty-seven piece Wilma Wolverine marching band.

Baton twirling is a step in the right direction and all part of my three-year plan. Last year, I worked hard on my grades. A girl with goals has to get good grades. This year, I'm concentrating on my social development. Next year, I'll try for something in student government.

It's serious business, but not to Daddy Dean.

He has changed since his surgery. When they removed his cancer, I think they took a slice of his ambition. He has always known how to have a good time. But he used to go to meetings now and then when he belonged to the Toastmasters, the Park Board, the service clubs. He used to start projects and finish them quicker than Mama could say, "Slow down!" Now he takes his sweet time over every little thing. Now he tells *me* to slow down. He even skipped the big Lions Club convention this year. "Too much hoopla," was his excuse. "I like summer in Wilma."

Summer in Wilma is hot and still and heavy with the smell of rotting pea vines. That's enough for Daddy Dean?

Sometimes I wonder if he's going to spend the rest of his life pounding nails and sipping tea and making remarks about the weather.

"Felt a drop," he says.

Sure enough, a cloudburst is on the way. I won't be twirling fire in the rain.

I glare at Mama, but it's nature's fault, really. Nature doesn't care about my plans. And much as I love him, I have to admit: Daddy Dean doesn't understand how important it is for me to *be* somebody.

Chapter 2

Daddy Dean is trying to separate the slippery days of summer.

"Make the most of each one," he tells me at breakfast. He's been saying things like that, since his cancer scare. "Seems like only yesterday we finished the deck," he adds wistfully, "and now July is over."

"Yep," I say, puzzled by the sadness in his voice. He mourns the passing of a month while I bask in the blending of my summer days.

August is the peak of Foamy's business year. We're all working double shifts. While Bud sizzles stacks of burgers on the back grill, Poe washes mugs and tries to keep up with the beverage orders. Arlene hangs reader board letters for our ice cream FLAVR of the MONTH: Lemon Sherbet.

I wait on customers.

My money changer bumps against my leg, kachinking in time to each quick footstep. I stop at a car full of boys and hope they won't notice the drop of perspiration sliding past my earlobe.

I brace myself when I see the driver, Edward "Animal" Gates, fullback on the football team.

"Full back, empty head," Poe says of him. He leers at me.

"What would you like?" I ask.

"I'd like a carhop to go with nothing on it."

"I'll have the same." From the back seat, I hear the cackles of James "Jumbo" Johnson and Carlos "Meat" Mendez.

Poe would be able to quiet them with a razor-sharp comment. I haven't her talent for cutting. What's more, I'm remembering that Animal Gates belongs to Leeza Sutter and Leeza Sutter belongs to the Cats. The Cats and the KOs are *the* clubs for junior and senior girls. Part of my three-year plan is to join one. But first I have to be invited.

So I hold my pencil over my order pad and wait. I try to look cheerful. Maybe Animal will think I'm a good sport. Maybe he'll tell Leeza.

"Hey, Baby-face, what's the holdup? The sign says fast service." Animal sticks his raw-knuckled hand out the window and tries to pinch me.

Arlene has told us to walk away from situations like this. "My girls don't have to take guff off anyone," she always says. But Arlene is fifteen feet up the ladder, still working at the reader board. I don't want to walk away, anyway. I want to make a good impression. I take a step backwards.

"Three root beers to go," Animal says, sullen-voiced and disgusted-looking.

When I place the order at the counter, I discover Poe has been watching.

She pours the root beer, snaps on the plastic lids, jabs a straw into each one. She hands them

10

to me in a white paper bag. "You should have told them off."

"I didn't want to lose my tip," I joke.

"Good grief, Wray Jean. You're a carhop, not a hooker."

"Relax, will you? I was only kidding." Mama's right, I guess, about Poe taking it easier.

She raises a fist and shakes it at Animal.

I push her hand back inside the window. I'm afraid she'll do worse. "Stop it," I beg. "Arlene might see you. Then you'll never be assistant manager."

Poe stands above the sink. She dips a dirty mug into the dishwater. "Give me a break," she drawls. "You're not worried about my job."

Of course I'm not. Poe is one of those people who gets away with murder. She'll be promoted one day no matter what trouble she triggers. She doesn't have to worry about things the way I do.

"I just don't want them to think . . ." I begin.

Poe wrings her washrag as if she's trying to strangle the soapy life out of it. "*They* don't care what *you* think." She twists harder.

Someday people will care what I think. That's good enough for me. I deliver the drinks without sharing this thought with Poe.

"That'll be one-eighty," I say.

Animal stretches back to reach into his pocket. He pulls up some change and tosses it out the window, past my hand, past the white paper bag.

I go stark blank for a moment, watching the coins fly by. Part of me wants to throw the root beer in his face. Part of me whispers "be careful, be careful, be nice." The money doesn't matter to

11

me. But what if I want to be a Cat? What if this is some kind of test?

"Oops," I say finally, as though it's all an accident. I bend to collect the coins, turning my face away in case it looks as red-hot as it feels. Gravel digs into my knee each time I press it down for balance.

Suddenly I hear Poe beside me, yelling. "Get the flaming blazes out of here!"

Bud is right behind her. "And don't come back," he hollers.

Animal's screeching away leaves a patch of rubber and a cloud of stinking exhaust. "BYE RITA!" he shouts to me. "See ya 'round!"

"Rita?" I say slowly. He doesn't even know who I am. I look up at Poe. "My name isn't Rita."

Poe snorts in disgust. "I call you *Hopeless*." I watch her stalk back inside. That's just like Poe—defend me, then leave me crouching in the parking lot.

"Let the money be," Bud says. "We don't want it." He offers his hand.

As I pull myself up, I see Arlene clambering down the ladder. Changing the reader board always puts her in a foul mood.

"I'd better get to the customers," I say.

Bud glances at Animal's old space where a blue station wagon is rolling to a stop. "Back to the burgers," he says.

I close my fingers around the few gritty coins I've gathered. I jingle them as I approach the station wagon. The boy inside looks familiar. I've seen him hanging around Beverly Benson and some other girls from the KO club. He plays baseball.

"Hi, Wray Jean," he says. "How about a large root beer? Please?"

"Coming right up," I tell him. At least someone knows my name. Trouble is, I can't think of his. I feel bad. Exchanging names is like exchanging presents. If someone knows yours, you want to return the favor. But I'd rather not insult him with the wrong name. Like "Rita," I think.

Poe knows him. She fills a tall mug and presses a straw to the side. "Bill Burnett. Nice guy. Always leaves a tip. *On* the tray."

I slide Animal's coins into my money changer. Two dimes and a bent nickel clunk into place. I ignore Poe's comment, but it turns out to be true. Bill Burnett leaves his change on the tray.

"Enjoy your root beer, Bill," I tell him. He grins when I say his name.

I hear Bud call "order out" for the third time. And Arlene is on the prowl, looking for someone to yell at.

I hurry to a car at the other end of the lot. On my way back, Bill blinks his lights. That's what the sign says, Blink Lights for Service. But most people just honk their horns. Why can't everyone be polite like Bill, I wonder.

The world is not a perfect place. Uncle Raymond announced this during our family dinner last Thanksgiving. Mama said it was her first clue as to his deteriorating condition. Probably because it wasn't like him to be the least bit pessimistic. His statement, however, was correct. If the world *were* a perfect place, I wouldn't have to grovel to impress the likes of Animal Gates.

Chapter 3

I have the day off today, for the first time this whole hot August. My windows are open, but there isn't enough breeze to flutter a feather, let alone my bedroom curtains. I flip through the pages of last year's annual, the Wilma Wolf Trap. *Another great year! Wolverines forever! Biology— I'll never forget it!*

I'm memorizing the smiling annual-picture faces of Shelly Adams, Tom Appling, Walter Benzel. I recognize Bill Burnett from Foamy's. Light brown hair, freckles, easy to forget.

"Don't for-get Bill Bur-nett," I chant.

Uncle Raymond always said a person should turn adversity into advantage. Every summer for the past ten years, he's come to Wilma for a two-week stay, telling stories of his setbacks and recoveries like some uncles tell fairy tales. Kayla calls them Raymond's Fables. But they're true. Once, when we visited him in Raleigh, we saw his real estate signs hanging all over the place. He was a success. I met his fiancée that trip. What a beauty. Not too smart, though. She married someone else. Then Uncle Raymond had his breakdown, or whatever you want to call it. I thought he would bounce right back. But I guess it's going to take more than a few months of rest and relaxation. "I've lost everything that's important to me," he told Daddy Dean. I suppose he meant his business and his money. But he'll make a comeback. I just know it. I remember every piece of advice Uncle Raymond ever gave me, including the one about adversity and advantage.

The way I look at it, Animal did me a favor by calling me "Rita," because he got me to thinking about names and how important they are. In September, when school starts, I'll know everyone's name. Maybe then, they'll want to know mine. Wray Jean Child, Helen Cox, Harvey Criddle . . .

Just as I get to the D's, Mama calls. "If you want me to hem that uniform, you'd better get yourself out here, Wray Jean."

"Coming," I shout. I leave the annual open on my desk and slip into my new white majorette uniform.

The head majorette wears a blue stripe around each cuff. The other twirlers wear plain cuffs. I look at my wrists and remember how badly I wanted these stripes. I practiced every spare moment and smiled, smiled, smiled through the spring tryouts even though Daddy Dean was going into the hospital the very next week.

"I don't know why you want this," he told me, "but I hope you get your wish." I think he understood me better then, before the surgery.

"Wray Jean!"

I can tell by Mama's tone she won't wait much longer. I pull on my tasseled boots and clomp to the kitchen.

16

"Stand up here," Mama says, patting the table. A row of straight pins sticks out of her mouth. They waggle when she talks.

I tap my toes to a drum roll in my head.

"Hold still," she commands. "How short do you want it?"

I touch my thigh, watching her. "Here?"

"Hmmmph," Mama grunts. She thinks that's too short, but she measures from where I've pointed anyway.

I hear Daddy Dean on the back stairs. He smiles when he sees me. But when he looks at my skirt, his lips turn down and his eyebrows knot up. Boots on the table don't bother him. This is his boys/driving/daughter-growing-up frown.

"Too short," he barks.

"Daddy Dean, we haven't even started!" I laugh, hoping he'll laugh, too. And change his mind.

"Too damn short." He captures my attention with his fierce glance. "I mean it."

My eyes weasel out from under his scowl. I sigh a calculated sigh—loud enough to record my frustration, but not so obvious as to bring on an argument.

Mama waits until Daddy Dean leaves the room before placing the first pin. She'll catch it from him later on. I look down at the top of her head, at the part weaving its way through her hair. I want to pat her head or stroke it, but we don't touch, Mama and I. I concentrate on standing straight and not wiggling, on making her job easier. That is my unspoken thank-you.

The phone rings just as Mama finishes. She

17

reaches for the receiver and her cigarettes at the same time.

"Hello?" she says. She waves me off the table, motioning toward the living room. I step-shuffle-step on in to find her an ashtray.

When I come back, she mouths the name "Raymond." Mama has said that sometimes he's too depressed to even dial our number. I am glad to think he is having one of his better days.

"Good, good," Mama says into the phone. "We've missed you, too. Maybe next summer . . . Yes. You just get to feeling better, hear?"

"How is he?" I ask, after she hangs up.

She blows out a stream of smoke. "He's happy there. The folks at Hearthaven are nice to him. All he ever wanted was for everyone to like him." She mashes her cigarette into the ashtray. "Lord knows why," she grumbles.

I know why, but my logic doesn't hold water with Mama.

I march back to my room, performing my parade routine with an invisible baton. I change out of my uniform and hang it on the doorknob of the little guest room Mama uses for sewing. Then I hurry back to my desk and pick up the annual again. When I come to Rusty's picture, I think of Daddy Dean's fierce frowning. His road map for me has only one-way streets. Lots of stoplights. No intersections. That's what I wrote to Kayla last week. She wrote back, "Same old Daddy Dean. Same old map."

I guess that's why he doesn't take to Rusty the way everybody else does. I mean, what's not to like? Rusty's no letterman or anything, but only because Wilma High doesn't have a rodeo team. Summer and fall, he straddles his papa's horses when he's not riding the harvest combines. I figure that's where he gets his stiff-legged walk. Thinking about the way Rusty moves makes my stomach shrink all up. As I tried to explain to Kayla in my letter: With Rusty, I imagine complicated detours off Daddy Dean's straight-and-narrow road. If I ever admitted that to Daddy Dean, he would ground me for life.

As if to remind me of this fact, his table saw growls from the basement like a watchdog. I hear it bite a board in two with a clipped-off yelp.

Rusty and Daddy Dean are making it impossible to concentrate. With a last look at Higgins, Hoover and Hulsey, I head down to the workshop.

A sawdust fog hangs in the air. Through it, I see a blurry version of my father bending over his workbench. He designed me a bookcase last spring, after Mama complained about the books stacked on my bedroom floor. It's meant for a belated birthday present, since he was in the hospital on my real birthday in April. I told him my present was his making it through surgery okay. But he drew up these plans anyway. Now, he is studying them. He is in a good mood. I know, because he is whistling his tinker's tune—no melody, just a blowing out of breath.

Daddy Dean has always found contentment among these rows of saws and screwdrivers and in the orderly progression of drill bits, sockets, nail-filled baby food jars. This afternoon, he welcomes me with a sheet of sandpaper. I clip it onto the electric sander and start to work. I like breathing

19

in the warm woodchip smell and feeling the sander's vibrations tingling in my hand. I don't really need the bookcase. Working alongside Daddy Dean is a gift in itself.

When I turn off the sander, the silence, too, is soothing. But it doesn't last long. I hear a far-off ringing and, soon after, Mama's voice.

"Wray Je-eean! Tellll-a-phone!"

I wipe my hands on my cut-offs. "I'll be right back," I promise.

"I'll be waiting," Daddy Dean says.

The stairs rise out of the basement's cool darkness into the bright summer heat. At the top I am out of breath, as much from the change in temperature as from the quick climb.

Mama has come in from her garden to answer the phone. She pulls on a dirt-crusty glove. "Your boyfriend," she says, louder than necessary.

Rusty wants me to go swimming.

"I'm helping my Dad," I tell him.

"You can always help your Dad," he complains, "but I won't have another day off for weeks."

"Yes, but . . ." I begin. But Daddy Dean expects me back. I see Rusty's side of it, too. I hate choosing between them.

"Everybody will be there, at the pool," Rusty says.

"Everybody?" I ask. Will Shelly Adams be there, I wonder, and Walter Benzel and all the Cats and all the KOs?

"Everybody," Rusty answers.

"I'll be ready in ten minutes," I say.

Daddy Dean looks disappointed when I tell him

I'm leaving for the afternoon. But he's a good sport about it. "Have fun with your friends," he says.

Upstairs, I soap the sawdust off my hands and roll a bath towel around my swimming suit. I comb my hair and brush my teeth and rub a drop of perfume between my wrists. Then I powder my face with blusher even though it will wash away in the chlorinated water of the city pool. I check the mirror to see that I look just right for Rusty and for the others.

In the background, the table saw whines and the sander buzzes on, without me.

Chapter 4

September's FLAVR of the MONTH is Blackberry. Daddy Dean drops by after work to have himself a cone and to toast the end of summer.

"August went so fast," he says. "But I guess you're glad to be back in school."

I nod, pleased and embarrassed at the dollar tip he offers me.

"Best service I've ever had," he says. When he drives away, he leaves a parking lot filled with kids this Indian summer afternoon. School started yesterday, on the third. The family trade has all but disappeared. Bud is selling fewer burgers and more onion rings.

Arlene looks critically at my uniform. She's leaving soon for her weekly appointment at the Beauty Bungalow, but not before she scrutinizes my root beer brown jumper and my vanilla milkshake white blouse. My vanilla sleeve has a chocolate stain on it. Who cares, I think, as I deliver two large floats. Arlene is so picky.

Beverly Benson rolls her window up enough so I can hang the tray on it. Page Miller reaches across her to pay me. "My treat," she tells Beverly. "And keep the change, Wray Jean," she adds.

"We've been watching you," says Beverly. "Your feet must be killing you, the way you run back and forth. Aren't you dead by the time you go home?"

"I guess I'm used to it," I say. It's nice for them to notice, though. Beverly is always looking out for people. And Page has this quirky sense of humor. They're both members of the National Honor Society, as well as belonging to the KO club. I'd feel a whole lot smarter if I were in National Honor Society.

As I leave their car I feel more intelligent already. Funny how some people can do that to you. Uncle Raymond used to make me feel that way. An hour with him was always good for two full days of confidence and optimism.

"EEE-yow!" Animal Gates howls from his car at the far end of the parking lot. Speaking of intelligence, I think sarcastically.

I turn to see Leeza Sutter's yellow convertible circle the drive-in.

"EEE-yow!" Leeza shouts back. "Hey, Animal! Hi, cutie!" She pulls into the stall in front of the order-out window. Adrian Neil and Linda Banes ride in the back seat. Merrilee Moore sits in front, looking sheepish.

I take a deep breath and try to walk casually toward them, pretending I don't know they're watching me. I clear my throat and smile. How do I look? I wonder. I notice the chocolate stain on my sleeve. It seems to have gotten bigger.

"May I help you?" I ask.

They laugh. "No," says Leeza, "but we can help you!" Her words are punctuated by a loud

23

cheering from the back. "Yyyyyaaa-whoooooo."
Arlene has left by now for her hair appointment
and I'm glad. She won't put up with kids
shouting. Says it scares away the real customers,
the grown-ups. I see Bud standing behind Poe with
his spatula in his hand. He'll want me to tell them
to keep it down.

"Um," I begin. "Well . . ."

"Cat got your tongue?" Adrian's mouth goes
wide with laughter. Then she hands me an
envelope. The others start singing:

We are the Cats. Meow-Meow
We are the best and how!
Every boy wants to pet a Cat
'Cause there's not a dog among us.
Just watch out you might get
Sssssscratched.

All together, they give the Cats hand signal.
Four claws rake the air.

My own hand trembles as I realize I am holding
an invitation! The best girls club wants *me* to join!
Their members are all the things I'm not—
gorgeous, popular, fun.

Linda waves another envelope in the air.
"Poe!" she shouts.

The others take up the chant. "Poe, Poe, Poe."

But Poe shakes her head and points to Bud,
beside her.

Linda shoves Poe's invitation into my hand.
"You deliver, 'kay?"

Leeza backs out while the others sing. "We are
the Cats, Meow-Meow. We are the best, and

how!'' I wave to everyone but Merrilee, who has scrunched down in her seat, out of sight.

"They want us!" I inform Poe, when I reach the window. "They want us both!"

I rip open my envelope. Inside is a cat-shaped card. "Congrats! You have been chosen to be a Cat. Initiation night Saturday, October 19. SSSsssssee you there."

Poe pushes out an order of three super fries. I tuck my invitation in the pocket of my jumper. They want me. I can hardly believe it.

I deliver the fries to Animal, Jumbo and Meat. "Thank-you, Wray Jean," they say in singsong unison. They're teasing, but in a different, flirtier way than before. And they know my name now. I wait for the money toss, but it doesn't come. Just three crisp dollar bills and the flash of a brown beer bottle before they drive away.

When I return to the counter, Beverly Benson is there, talking with Poe.

"Did I forget something?" I ask.

"No," Beverly says quietly. "*I* did." She hands us each an envelope—a KO invitation, I realize. Then she gestures gracefully in the general direction of Leeza's car. "I couldn't help noticing," she remarks, her cheeks dimpling. "You have a choice to make."

"Oh. Yes! Thank-you!" I say, trying to match her sincere manner.

As soon as she is back in her car, I read the KO invitation: "We would be pleased to have you as a member of the KOs. Initiation ceremonies are Saturday, October 19. We hope you will accept."

A choice.

When I think of the two clubs, I know immediately where I would best fit in, where I would feel most comfortable. But I have to be firm with myself. I have to remind myself that comfort isn't my goal in life. Challenge is, and change. The question I have to ask myself is this: Which club will help me become the Wray Jean I want to be?

By eight o'clock the parking lot starts to empty. A rack full of mugs drips and dries in the cooling night air. Poe and I face each other through the walk-up order window. We pull out our invitations.

"Well?" I ask. "What are you going to do?"

Poe rolls her eyes. "Do you really have to ask?"

True, I think. We both know what's best for us.

"It's not even a choice," Poe says.

We hold our invitations, one in each hand, and tap them on the counter—1,2,3, like when we were growing up together, playing Paper/Scissors/Rock. The winner gave the loser slaps on the wrist: *Paper wraps rocks.* Sometimes we'd wet our fingers first. *Scissors cut paper.* A quick slap would hurt more than a slow one. *Rock smashes scissors.* We'd clench our teeth and pretend it didn't hurt.

1,2,3,—we raise our invitations.

Poe holds up her KO card.

I hold up my Cat's.

We stare at each other as if we are strangers, as if we knew each other once but can't remember when or where.

"Girls," Bud says gently, "there's a customer."

Oh, how those slaps used to sting.

Chapter 5

A School Leader Sets a Good Example.

The words stand out white against the blackboard. Mr. Sharp, our school activities director, has practically carved them into the surface.

He is lecturing this Friday morning on behalf of the School Leadership Council. Fifty-six of us copy down the date—September 6—and his words, caps and all. Because if you want to do anything important at Wilma High, you've got to belong to SLC. A non-member can't run for office or be a varsity cheerleader or captain of any team, athletic *or* academic.

Poe, sitting beside me, taps her thumbs together. I sense her eagerness. We're all fresh from vacation. It seems as though new opportunities lie at our feet like Mama's summer squash, growing bigger each day, just waiting to be harvested. Mr. Sharp is fresh, too. His face is tanned. The pens lining his shirt pocket gleam shiny under the fluorescent lights.

"How does one set a good example?" he asks.

Beverly Benson raises her hand. "Participation?"

Mr. Sharp nods.

Two more hands shoot up.

"Grade point."

"Grooming."

My stubborn brain won't produce a single idea. By the time I come up with "self-discipline," Mr. Sharp has moved on to the point system.

"In future meetings, you will learn the various ways of earning points. Based on the totals, the final forty-five members of the Student Leadership Council will be selected in April in time for next year's student body elections."

Chairs creak as people shift in their seats. One or two throats grumble clear. Otherwise, it is quiet in the student activities room. The limit is scary. But it adds to the challenge, I guess. It makes everyone work a little harder.

Poe scribbles something on her paper. 45??? she writes. "Excuse me," she says, after Mr. Sharp ignores her waving hand. "Why can't there be room for everyone? Why not set a point limit instead of a person limit?"

If it were *me* and Mr. Sharp ignored *my* hand, I would bring it down quick and neat so as not to create a scene. I would lower my hand and keep my mouth shut. Never complain, never explain. This was one of Uncle Raymond's mottos and not a bad one, either. It's hard enough to earn your way into SLC without being a troublemaker.

Poe presses on. "Why a limit at all?"

"I have my reasons," Mr. Sharp says. The bell rings. He seems to expect everyone to jump up and leave. We don't. I, for one, am interested in his reasons.

"What are they?" Poe asks.

"They are indisputable," he answers. He folds his binder shut and walks out the door.

Poe's face reddens. Her jaw muscles jut out.

"If his reasons were any good, he'd tell us," I whisper.

Poe nods. Her question was valid and we both know it.

I sniff my best prim-and-proper etiquette sniff. "Mr. Sharp certainly doesn't set a mannerly example." I am glad to see the tightness leave Poe's face.

After school, I go to majorette practice and earn two points for participation.

When I tell Daddy Dean about the meeting, he wrinkles his nose. He is lounging on the couch with his shoes off and his feet up. He looks like I do when I am pretending his socks smell. "Why don't you set a good example by getting me something to drink?" he asks.

I tickle his big toe. "One cold beer, coming up."

He shakes a mocking finger my way. "School leaders don't serve alcohol. How about a glass of milk instead?"

"Milk?" On hot days like today, Daddy Dean likes a beer after work. I wonder if he's being sarcastic. His face tells me "no." I pour the milk and fill a bowl of nuts to go with it. I pick out all the cashews for myself. He doesn't like them. "Maybe we could work on the bookcase tonight," I call from the kitchen.

"Sounds good," he calls back. But by the time I juggle everything into the living room, he is asleep, snoring medium-loud and steady.

I put his milk back in the refrigerator and carry my cashews to the bedroom, to munch while I review my notes.

A School Leader Follows School Rules.

This is the theme of Mr. Sharp's Friday the thirteenth lecture. I don't think there's a connection. My notebook is filling up with Mr. Sharp's SLC guidelines. There are fifty-five of us now. Poe has dropped out in protest. Actually, she didn't exactly drop out. "A good leader must be a good follower," Mr. Sharp told her in the hallway last week. "That doesn't make sense," she argued. "Perhaps you should extend your efforts elsewhere," he suggested. "Perhaps you should use mouthwash," she replied.

I offered to quit, but I guess Poe could sense that I didn't really want to. Mr. Sharp may be difficult, but he calls the shots at Wilma High. "It's okay to want different things," Poe told me. "Besides, we're friends, not Siamese twins."

Fridays, Poe gets to eat a leisurely breakfast, while I sit in the student activities room from seven A.M. to eight-fifteen. This morning, under School Rules, Mr. Sharp writes: *Appearance, Attendance, No Outside Clubs.*

Most of us dress according to the SLC's unwritten standards. Hardly anyone skips classes. The rule that Mr. Sharp has never been able to enforce is the one banning outside clubs. He says they exclude people and cause hurt feelings. I say he can't control them, so he wants to pretend they don't exist. I'm not an official member of the Cats yet—"you're just a Kitten until initiation," they told me—but in spite of Mr. Sharp's warning, I intend to join. Everybody does it.

As I gather my things after the meeting, Connie Frost, another Kitten, stops by my desk. "Do you have the Snakes album?"

I shake my head. I've never heard of them, but I don't tell her that.

"It's the best," she decrees. "Get it."

After school, I hurry to the music store. Rules within rules, I think, as I hand the cashier my tip money from last weekend. There are even rules about which music to listen to, if you want to be somebody at Wilma High.

We've never had many formal rules at our house. The main one is being on time for dinner. Daddy Dean likes us to eat together. "My favorite time of day," he always says. When I get home, I pull the new album from its cardboard sleeve and try to guess what we'll have tonight. Seems like the spice has gone out of Mama's cooking. She's been serving boiled potatoes, applesauce, macaroni and cheese. I miss her stuffed green peppers and Daddy Dean's favorite, red hot tamales. "We need a new bottle of hot sauce," I told her the other day. "No we don't," she said. She pointed to a mimeographed list on the kitchen bulletin board. I read the heading—Bland Foods. "Why?" I asked. "Healthier," she said. *Boring,* I thought. But the way she started banging pots around, I wasn't about to say it.

I leave my bedroom door open a crack so I'll hear Mama's call. Then I plant myself cross-legged in front of the stereo. I set the needle to the outside groove and try to figure out why the

31

Snakes are "the best." Words blare out, but I can't understand them. The music is loud and pulsing. I want to like it, but I don't. I play it a second time, in case I missed something.

I'm halfway through Side Two when I notice Daddy Dean filling the narrow space in my doorway.

"Dinner?" I ask, smiling up at him.

He doesn't answer, doesn't even smile back. What's wrong? I wonder. What has happened? His eyes are bloodshot. Anger pinches his face. Daddy Dean has never looked at me like this before. He never *would*. I don't get it, I want to say, but my mouth is frozen shut. His glance touches on the record player before he slams the door. The reverberation travels through the floorboards and up into my bones. It travels to my hand, which is still shaking when I reach over to lift the needle. The record protests its scratching loudly, then spins round and round in silence as though it, too, is stunned.

I am still staring at the door when Mama opens it. "You had loud music on?" she asks.

"That's all," I complain. "What's wrong with *him?*" I expect her to tell me he's just had a bad day, that he'll get over it.

"No more," she says instead. "Keep it down. Better yet, don't play it at all."

A new rule. No Snakes in the house.

"He can't sleep," Mama explains.

Why is he sleeping in the afternoons anyway? Maybe I don't want to know.

Chapter 6

It doesn't take a genius to figure out things are different around here. They changed sometime during the busyness of early September, when I wasn't paying attention. Mama, who used to make great chili, cooks creamed rice casseroles. Daddy Dean, who used to dance to the radio, slams doors against music. Against me.

I guess Friday the thirteenth really is bad luck because ever since then, things have been going downhill.

Monday, Daddy Dean didn't join us for dinner. "He had a big lunch," Mama told me. "What about this being his favorite time of day," I asked, after clearing the table. "Hand me that SOS," she said. I think she scoured every pan in the kitchen.

Tuesday, Daddy Dean didn't go to work. "He couldn't sleep again last night," Mama explained. "Maybe because of his afternoon naps," I suggested. Mama didn't answer. She was busy squirting ammonia on the windows and polishing them with crumpled newspaper.

Wednesday, Mama moved into the little guest room next to mine. "Your father kicks in his sleep," she informed me. "I was awake all night." "So you're moving out?" I asked. She wiped a damp cloth over the light switch by the guest room door. "These walls need washing," she complained.

Thursday, Mama and I sat over morning coffee, sipping from the pottery mugs Uncle Raymond made us last Christmas. "Is everything okay?" I asked. Daddy Dean was sleeping in, skipping work another day. Mama seemed half-asleep herself. "Is everything okay?" I asked again. "There's no need to get upset," she assured me. "I don't want you to worry." When I left for school, she was rearranging cupboards.

Today, Friday, September 20, I dress for school, trying to be quiet, trying to follow the new house rules. Mama doesn't want me to worry. But surely I'm not the only one to wonder. It must have crossed Mama's mind. Daddy Dean must have asked it himself. Hard as I try to push it away, the question keeps coming back to me.

Did they get it all?

It. Cancer. The unspoken word spins out like a spider's thread, thin and sticky, stretching and connecting, until all of us are caught in it.

Did they get it all? Dr. Peck said so. Mama said so. Daddy Dean believed it, too. "I'm going to lick this thing," he vowed last April.

Through my door, and his, I plead with him. Get up. Go to work. You don't belong in bed.

Then again, maybe that's how he plans to lick it—with lots of rest and bland food and no loud music.

Then again, if they got it all, what's to lick?

"They didn't get it all, did they?" I confront Mama on the basement stairs. She is wielding a cloth-covered broom, trying to sweep a nasty-looking cobweb from the stairwell ceiling.

She acts as though she hasn't heard me. I'm not surprised. I know Mama's ways. I don't expect her to say, "Yes, Wray Jean, the cancer is back." I don't expect her to say the word out loud. But I know she won't lie to me, much as she tries to pretty up the truth at times.

Her silence is her answer.

"What do we do now?" I ask.

"Hope for the best," Mama says, vaguely. "There's always hope."

On my way to school, I think of hope. I think of Mama, jabbing at a stubborn thread of cobweb, a dark thread, black from summer dust and seemingly unreachable.

Chapter 7

A School Leader Is a Team Player.

"This means," says Mr. Sharp, "that a school leader puts the good of others above his own interests."

Do I do that, I wonder, as I try to stifle a yawn. Daddy Dean was up wandering again last night. I was awake until 3 A.M. "September 27," I write in my notebook—"Put the good of others above your own."

School has been in session less than a month. Already, I have joined the Girls' League and the Glee Club. Just last week, I signed up for Future Teachers of America because it is led by my favorite teacher, Mr. Page. I spend my free time painting posters and baking cookies for school functions. I almost wish I weren't on so many committees. Sometimes, like this morning, when I'm slumped down in my chair at the forty-ninth meeting of the week, I think, "What am I doing it for?" Times like these, I tell myself, "Wray Jean, this is going to look awfully good on your résumé," and that perks me right up. Clubs are important stepping stones on the road to becoming the Wray Jean I want to be.

I get tired, though.

36

"You need your rest," Mama says, when I get home.

"You, too," I tell her. I don't think she sleeps well in that little guest room.

Mama has taken a leave of absence from her volunteer job at the library. In the mornings, she drives Daddy Dean to the clinic for tests. Later, she fixes his lunch, then leaves him alone to sleep the rest of the day away. "I want to be here if he needs me," she says.

She is folding sheets this afternoon. "He can do without bedsores," she murmurs with a frown. I hold one end of a contour sheet while she shakes it flat at the other. "Oh!" she says, remembering something good. "He ate lunch in the kitchen today."

I imagine her coaxing Daddy Dean out of his room to sit at the table. She coaxes a lot lately.

Sometimes I hear him snap at her. I hear her reply, pleasant and calming. She never snaps back. But she comes out of the bedroom and I see her face, flushed, and her eyes bright with tears. If she catches me staring, she puts on a different face. She smiles. She explains away his crabbiness. "He's tired today. He had a hard night."

Then she goes to her room. And I, to mine. In and out. Across the hall. The waltz of the closing doors.

But today Daddy Dean got up. A good sign.

When we finish folding the sheets, Mama says, "Let's have a snack. I made tapioca."

She takes care of everyone. A Team Player. Mr. Sharp would like that.

* * *

A School Leader Communicates.

"Communication is comprised of two parts: talking and listening. One without the other is not communication."

It strikes me that Mr. Sharp has talked all of September and now into the first Friday of October. We have been doing all the listening these past five weeks. Is that what he means by communication?

Daddy Dean and I have always communicated well. We just do it differently now. After school, I sit on a hard, straight-backed chair by his bed. I offer him scraps of my day. I ask him how he is feeling. "Oh, not so bad," he tells me, or like today, "Oh, not so good."

Dr. Peck has been here before me. His visits are becoming a regular part of Daddy Dean's life. Mama keeps saying, "Thank God he's a family friend. How many doctors make house calls any more?" I'm grateful he comes, but when he tried explaining the test results, I ignored him. He was wrong once, about getting it all. He could be wrong again, about it spreading. Daddy Dean will get his strength back, one of these days.

I see that I am tiring him. Before I go, he reaches out to me. We touch, palm to palm. He squeezes. I squeeze back. That is the communication part. Our ritual.

"Communication leads to understanding," Mr. Sharp told us this morning. I don't understand why this had to happen to Daddy Dean. I don't understand how he ended up stuck in this darkened room. But for these few seconds of hand holding, the drawn green curtains fade away. The celery green walls disappear. The white bedspread and flowered carpet melt into the background of another time, a better time, when Daddy Dean tucked *me* in and kissed *me* goodnight.

Demerits.

"I have saved the best for last," Mr. Sharp tells us this Friday, October 11. You might even call him jaunty this morning, the final session of the SLC lectures.

"By now, you know how to earn points. But there are ways to lose them, too. I call them the four F's.

Animal Gates has a coughing fit in the back row. Mr. Sharp waits until he can control himself before continuing.

"Fabricating, fighting, failing, and forgetting," he says.

I'm glad when he is finished. My notebook is full. Friday never felt so fine.

Saturday, Daddy Dean is at the kitchen table when I come to breakfast. He must be making an extra effort for Kayla, home for a surprise three-day visit.

I pour coffee while Mama stands over the frying pan. Daddy Dean used to be the weekend cook. Kayla and I would giggle at the funny animal-shaped pancakes he created. "I'm so hungry I could eat an elephant," we joked, hopefully. And in two minutes, there, on a platter, would appear an elephant with a curled-up trunk.

This morning, Mama brings us each a stack of perfectly round pancakes. She apologizes to Daddy

39

Dean. "I can't make fancy ones like yours." She means it as a compliment.

"That's okay," he says. "I'm so hungry, I could eat a . . . a circle!"

I push the butter knife gently through the soft cube of margarine. Daddy Dean has made a joke—a little anemic wisecrack. I chuckle politely. Daddy Dean looks surprised at himself. He chuckles, too. We snicker back and forth until Kayla and Mama join in, until we're all shaking with belly laughs. It's been so long. It feels so good.

Kayla has this funny laugh we've always teased her about. "Hoot-ee, hoot-ee," Daddy Dean imitates, setting us off again.

When we finally settle down to giggles and ahhhs, the pancakes are cold. But who cares? Daddy Dean eats only a few bites anyway. The laughing has worn him out.

"Good breakfast," he tells Mama. "Great. Really." He pushes his plate away, his stack of circles soggy with syrup.

He stands then, and heads for the door. His short cotton bathrobe exposes his legs. They startle me with their whiteness. I glance at Kayla. She is staring, wide-eyed, at Daddy Dean's back. We are thinking the same thing. He's so skinny! When did this happen? I wonder. My food sticks in midswallow. When did he get so thin and so pasty? He walks away on his spindly legs. I can't watch.

Mama rises as if to follow him. But he doesn't like her to hover. So instead, she pours more coffee.

I examine the family of mugs Uncle Raymond gave us. That way, I don't have to think about anything else. Our names have been carved into each one: Mae, Wray Jean, Kayla, Dean. The mugs are made of thick pottery. They hold warmth and they give warmth. They are a lot like Uncle Raymond used to be, before he started working clay at Hearthaven. But everything is changing now. Mama worries that Uncle Raymond is more depressed than before, that reality is too harsh for him. She seems to be wrestling with her own truths. Daddy Dean wears his skin two sizes too big. Doesn't she notice? Or is she getting used to the changes? I can understand that. Try as I might, I can't remember when things were normal.

What a family. Fabricating. Fighting. Failing. Forgetting.

I have the feeling we are all losing points.

Chapter 8

"How's this?" Arlene hands me a small cone filled with October's FLAVR of the MONTH: Pumpkin.

The taste of cinnamon tickles my tongue. "Delicious," I say, "like cold pumpkin pie."

Bud and Poe lick their own cones. There's not a whole lot else to do. October doesn't bring many customers to Foamy's. "It's the chili-dog time of year," Bud quips. But he doesn't sell many chili dogs either. Outside, fog halos glow silver-gray around the streetlights. Inside, the grill fills the air with essence of onion.

Poe and I have just finished scrubbing every inch of the linoleum floor. With Daddy Dean being sick and with our different school projects, it seems like the only time we see each other anymore is at work.

My ice cream drips on the front of my official Foamy's sweater, a bulky orange cardigan Arlene picked out because the color reminded her of cheddar cheese. She practically leaps across the room to dab at the spot. Then she returns to her "office," a stool pulled up to an empty stretch of shelf. She reaches into a paper bag. I recognize the Sew & Sew store logo, a needle spearing a spool of thread.

"New outfits, *again?*" Bud asks.

"For summer!" Arlene pulls out five brightly colored Sew-Easy patterns and waves them at us. "We have to keep up appearances," she lectures. She puts the patterns on her shelf and pats her hair self-consciously. She dyed it red this fall because, she said, Bud always wanted to date a redhead. "She's turned with the trees," he tells everyone, proudly. The way Bud says it, it sounds like a line from a poem.

Arlene tucks a strand of leaf-colored hair behind one ear and begins to unfold a thin tissue-paper pattern. "Come on over, Wray Jean," she says. "Let's see how this looks on you." The picture on the envelope shows a short skirt and middy blouse.

"Popeye!" Poe cracks as Arlene lays the pattern for the sailor collar over my shoulders.

"You want to repeat that?" Arlene turns a hostile eye on Poe.

"Not before I have me spinach," Poe answers, deadpan.

Arlene snatches the collar away. "We've worked you two *silly!*" She smiles but there is a tightness in her voice. I think we've hurt her feelings. "If you don't care for this look, I have others." She shows us four new pictures. "Somewhere in here, there's got to be a pattern we all like."

"Don't count on it," Poe says under her breath.

Luckily, the rasping of Bud's grill-cleaning brick scrapes over her words.

I watch Arlene nibble at her fingernail while she tries to decide between the five summer outfits. I wish I could go to the Sew & Sew store and pick out a pattern for the Wray Jean I want to be—a Quickie Pattern I could cut out and sew up in an evening. I stare into the parking lot, imagining what it would look like. Two headlights turn toward the drive-in and blind me momentarily. I blink. The lights blink. It must be Rusty's car.

"Is that your ride, Baby?" Arlene checks the clock over the hot fudge warmer.

"Yeah, that's Rusty."

"Rusty?" she says, more interested now. "HI HANDSOME!" She mouths the words emphatically and waves through the window. I'd give odds Rusty is blushing. He cranks his window down and waves back.

"We haven't seen him around for a while." Arlene pouts, as though Rusty's been avoiding her on purpose.

I pull my jacket on. My sweater bunches in the sleeves. "He's been working the amateur rodeos. County Fairs kept him busy all September. I haven't seen much of him, either."

I grab the bag of stale buns Bud always saves for me. Poe wiggles her eyebrows, Groucho Marx style. "Feeding the ducks tonight?" she says wickedly.

"Shhhhh." Poe would just love to make some big deal out of a little fun and get Arlene and Bud all riled up over nothing.

"How's your daddy, by the way?" Bud asks.

"Oh, about the same." When people ask me about Daddy Dean, I try to figure out how much they want to hear. I could spend an hour telling Bud how Daddy Dean is, but since he didn't ask until I was ready to leave, he obviously doesn't want to hear an hour's worth. I wish someone did, though. It would feel good to talk. Letters to Kayla help, but I hold back. I don't want to upset her. Poe would listen, if Bud and Arlene weren't always around.

Arlene fills a plastic bowl with a spiral of soft ice cream. "Take some of this to him."

"Thanks," I say. "He'll like that."

"Bye, Kitten." Poe scratches the air, teasing me with the Cat signal.

"Bye, Slugger." I shake a fist twice, the official version of the KO Knock Out signal. Then, together, we rake the air with a fist in our own secret combination. We love knowing how the two clubs would hate it if they could see us. It must be against some rule or other to violate the integrity of the claw or the fist.

"I saw that," Rusty informs me, as I hop into his warm car. "I'm telling. And then the Cats will throw you out on your tail."

I groan at his corny pun. "I think I'll walk home," I say.

"I think I'll drive you," he insists. Thank goodness.

Rusty waits in the car while I go inside with the ice cream. Daddy Dean props himself against his pillows and samples a spoonful. He acts as though its the best thing he's ever eaten. After each bite, he closes his eyes and makes a little *mmmm* noise.

45

I feel glad and guilty at the same time. I know Daddy Dean wouldn't enjoy this at all if he knew Rusty and I had a date tonight, in the middle of the week.

We drive to Wildwood Park. The fog has cleared. The headlights beam over the pond and the path around it, outlining the fat ducks as they waddle toward us. Rusty grabs the bag of old hamburger buns.

"Wait," I say softly. Everybody's been asking "How's your father?" I just want someone to listen to the answer, for once.

"You know how my Dad's been sick?" I begin.

Rusty nods and flicks off his lights.

"Well, last spring, they didn't get it all. His, uh, cancer."

Rusty nods again. He doesn't seem surprised. He pulls me closer. Snuggled against the seams and buttons of his denim jacket, I ask, "What if he doesn't get better? What if . . . I'm afraid my father is going to . . ."

"Don't say it," Rusty interrupts. "Don't even think it. That's like admitting defeat before you've even started. Like throwing yourself on the ground before you've mounted the bronco."

I pull away from the roughness of Rusty's jacket. He treats life as if it were one long rodeo ride.

"Did I say something wrong?" he asks.

I shake my head. Maybe his cowboy wisdom makes sense. What good does it do to worry? No use letting negative thinking affect Daddy Dean's health. Think positive. That's what Uncle Raymond would say.

Or don't think at all, I tell myself. Just don't think.

"Let's go," I say. The ducks start quacking when Rusty opens his door. They follow us as we walk around the pond, holding hands and tossing chunks of bread. When the last crumbs are scattered, I head for the slide. The ladder rungs echo with each step. I take a deep breath at the top. When I sit, the metal coldness seeps through my jeans. I shiver, pushing off into the darkness. Sliding down feels like riding the wind on a hard shiny carpet. Rusty catches me at the bottom.

Later, he spins me on the merry-go-round until I am breathless. "Stop," I beg, feeling out of control. But I am laughing now, so Rusty keeps on pushing me in circles. Finally the merry-go-round slows and comes to a standstill. I walk toward the swings in a crazy, crooked line, bumping against Rusty on purpose.

He settles into the swing next to me. We glide peacefully, back and forth, together. Then his swing starts to sneak higher than mine. I pump harder. Sly Rusty pretends he doesn't notice. But he pumps harder, too. Soon our feet are pointing to the stars. The cold air brushes our faces, as if we are in flight. After the crest of every backswing, my body plummets. My stomach squeezes tight with a little thrill. It is a delicious feeling, a pumpkin ice cream with cinnamon feeling.

By the time we stop, my face is tingling with

the cold. Rusty leaps from his swing and stands before me in his gunslinger position.

"Stick 'em up," I say, imitating all the cowboy movies we've watched together. I stand and point my two-finger pistols at him. "Back away now, Pardner. Back, back away."

He raises his hands. "Don't shoot, little lady," he pleads.

"Don't make me," I threaten. I lower my guns to his feet. "Now dance!"

Rusty shuffles and jumps in his stiff way, as though I'm capable of twirling his spurs with my sharpshooting ability. Then, miraculously, he dodges my bullets and grabs my wrists.

"Drop 'em," he orders. When my hands go limp, he looks down at the ground and kicks my guns away with two smooth swipes of his beat-up boots. I can almost see the six-shooters skid out of reach.

I feel like a little kid, full of silliness and joy and something I can't describe. Ah, Rusty, I think, I love the way you play.

He catches me smiling to myself. "Now you stick 'em up," he says, gently.

He lifts his hands to mirror mine. I spread my fingers slightly and we touch, but just barely, fingertip to fingertip.

"Much obliged, M'am," he murmurs. His lips are still moving when they meet my mouth. I close my eyes and I am sliding again, and twirling and twirling and flying free.

Chapter 9

The bright lights of the football stadium blaze down on the marching band as we high-step onto the field at halftime. The Wolverines are ahead 7 to 3. Light bounces off the trumpets and tubas and trombones. It is chilly. When I take deep breaths to relax myself, I exhale puffs of fog.

Suddenly the spotlights go out. There is silence. Then the hollow rumbling of the kettle drum begins. My heartbeat matches the drum roll, louder and faster, until the murmuring of the crowd drowns out the pounding. A small flame appears before me, and then another. Mr. Sharp's face looms grotesque in the flickering shadows. He hands me my fire baton with a spooky smile.

The band plays "Hey, Look Me Over" while I trace complicated patterns in the night. I'm not cold anymore, but warm with the excitement of performing. It is one of those nights when the music and the movement and the magic work together. I know I can't miss. This confidence makes my performance even better. I end with a series of aerials. My spinning baton forms a circle of fire, rising and falling, higher and faster, until the flames are extinguished in mid-air. The lights come on after the last notes die out. The crowd applauds. I try not to smile too broadly. "Practice makes perfect," Uncle Raymond would say. When the magic comes, it makes all the practice worthwhile. I see Rusty in the audience, clapping and waving. I wish Mama and Daddy Dean could have been here.

Mr. Sharp takes my baton and drops it into its metal case. He pats my back when we reach the sidelines. In front of all the students and parents milling about, he says, "Well done, Wray Jean. You were a fine representative of Wilma High School tonight."

"Good job, cutie!" Adrian Neil elbows me and winks. "Ready for tomorrow?"

"I guess so," I say. I'm glad Mr. Sharp has turned the other way. It is Friday, October 18. Tomorrow night is the Cats' initiation.

On Saturday evening, I dress according to the list of regulations. Long underwear, cut-offs, an old shirt, a pair of rubber boots, a large onion tied around my neck with twine.

"Show Daddy Dean," Mama urges. "He'll get a kick out of it."

I open his door. He squints at me, puzzled. "Have fun," he says, as though he doesn't believe I will.

But how could I not have fun? Tonight is a milestone. After tonight, I will officially belong. The only bad part is that Poe won't be there with me. She'll be undergoing her own initiation into the KOs. I can't wait to compare notes. She sounded excited on the phone this afternoon. "Good luck," we told each other. And I do feel lucky. Right now, I feel as though I can have it all, as though the Wray Jean I want to be might really exist someday.

This thought cheers me on the drive to Wildwood Park. Once there, we ten Kittens kneel in the dirt, and wait. I've heard stories about initiation, so I'm not surprised when someone sneaks up behind me to pour molasses and corn syrup over my head. Faceless in the dark playground, the girls who make up the Cats are no longer individuals. They drop raw eggs down our long underwear and then squish them. "Meow!" they command. And we do, with pitiful little mewing noises, because it's cold out and the eggs are sliding slimy down our legs. "This will bring you closer," they say. "Going through initiation will make you a family. We don't want any cat fights." They are howling now, with laughter. I try, but I can't even bring up a chuckle. I wonder when the good part comes. I think I'm going to freeze out here, until they drape us in sheets and herd us into cars.

When we walk into the basement of Leeza Sutter's house, the heated air wraps around me like a welcoming hug.

"Don't drip on the floor, you pigs," someone shouts.

"Yeah, you're pigs, not Cats yet. Look how sloppy you are."

"Now you have to be punished. Everyone take a bite of your necklace."

The onion is strong. The oil burns my mouth. My eyes fill up, stinging.

"Another bite, you pigs!"

51

"You don't deserve to be Cats. Look how ugly you are!"

A mirror appears in front of me. I *am* ugly. A line of lipstick zig-zags around my mouth. Black goop runs down my forehead.

"One more test."

They blindfold us and take us, one by one, into another room.

When it's my turn, the chill of the playground comes back to me. I hold myself to keep from shivering.

"Kneel!" I am pushed to my knees on the hard cement floor. I put my hands out to catch myself and feel something cold and smooth.

I recognize Leeza's voice as it floats above me. "We can't get this to flush," she says. "You have to clean it out for us."

I pull my hand from the rim of the toilet bowl.

"Go ahead," someone else snarls, "we don't have all night."

"Maybe she doesn't really want to be a Cat."

"Hurry up or forget it."

"There's something in there we can't get rid of. Find it," Leeza commands.

I can't do it, I think. *Yes, you can.* Why did I want to be in this stupid club anyway? *Because they're the best.* Maybe if I can get through this part, things will get better. *That's right! The other Kittens must have done the same thing. You can do it, too.*

I slip my hand into the water and touch a softish lump. I retch, tasting raw onion. They wouldn't, I think. Would they?

"Take it out," Leeza says.

I lift it out, the water trickling noisily.

"Now," says Leeza, "eat it."

The mushy lump starts to slip from my fingers. I know, suddenly, there isn't going to be a good part to this night. Why should there be? Nothing this whole school year has turned out the way I thought it would. I try to hide the beginnings of a sob, humiliated by my shaking shoulders.

"What a crybaby."

"Yeah, eat it or we'll help you."

"Just one bite," a gentle voice says. I think it belongs to Merrilee Moore. Her kindness in the middle of all this shouting makes me cry harder.

"Shut up, Merrilee," someone says.

A rough hand shoves the thing to my face. I smell a familiar smell. Peanut butter. I can do this, I think, just to get it over with, just to get out of here. I take the tinest of bites. It's only peanut butter over a banana. Still, I gag as it goes down, thinking what it could have been.

As soon as I swallow, everyone starts cheering.

"See," chirps Leeza, "that wasn't so bad."

Suddenly arms are around me, hugging and patting. "We love you, Wray Jean! We love you! We love you!" Their voices are excited now. "You're one of us!" My arms hang heavy at my sides. I couldn't hug them back if I wanted to.

But when they remove my blindfold, I see they are genuinely happy I made it. Merrilee squeezes my shoulder. "I'm sorry," she whispers. She puts a paper towel in my hand and leads me into the family room.

The sudden light blinds me. As my eyes adjust, I see eight newly initiated Cats, faces filthy, eyes

53

timid. Bowls of uneaten popcorn and bottles of untouched pop are scattered over the floor. I sit waiting for the last new member to emerge from the bathroom. No one speaks until she stumbles in, red-eyed and blotchy-skinned. The room is full now, with all the Cats. "We are the Cats. Meow-Meow," we sing. They hand out more paper towels so we can wipe our faces. They give us red sweatshirts with "Cats" written on them and white claw marks slashed across the front. Slowly, I begin to remember how much I wanted this.

I wanted it and I've earned it.

As we get ready to leave, they say, "Don't tell anyone what went on tonight."

Who would I dare tell? I drive away to the sounds of their shouting.

"We love you! We love you!"

Through my numbness, a spark of excitement flickers and dies, flickers and burns, dies and flickers and burns.

I'm in.

Chapter 10

The bathroom light shines from the front of the house, welcoming me. I'm used to it being on all the time now, a night light of sorts, for Daddy Dean. I like it. It makes me feel secure.

"Hello?" I sing. "I'm home." No answer. Daddy Dean must be sleeping. Maybe Mama, too. I tiptoe down the hall toward my room, careful not to smear molasses on the walls. The bathroom door is closed. As I get closer, I hear Mama and Daddy Dean, laughing.

"Does that feel good?" Mama asks.

"Mmmm." Daddy Dean murmurs a low, contented sound. "It's getting cool, though," he says.

I have to strain to understand them. Then the water comes on and I can't make out a thing over the gushing, rushing, tub-filling noise. I know I shouldn't eavesdrop. But my feet won't carry me away. Then the faucet squeaks off.

"I'll get your neck," Mama says.

Water splashes quietly. I imagine a soft soapy washcloth, rubbing warm over Daddy Dean's back.

"I love you, Mae," he says. I catch my breath

at his words. I have never heard him talk that way to Mama.

"And I love you," she says.

I creep away to the sound of dripping water. I ache with a longing I can't name. It feels like when I was away at camp one summer, missing everyone and everything in Wilma. If I didn't know better, I'd say I was homesick. But that doesn't make sense. You're nuts, I tease myself, just like Uncle Raymond.

I rinse my clothes in the utility room, next to the basement shower. Boy, they stink. Someone plastered Limburger cheese all over my back. The smell stays in my hair even after I wash it three times.

I try to imagine the KOs' initiation. Maybe Poe is busy scrubbing herself clean right now, too.

The upstairs bathroom is empty when I finally head for bed. A sweet powdery scent drifts out into the hallway. Mama stirs in her little bedroom. "How'd it go?" she calls softly.

"Well," I say, "I'm in."

"That's nice," she answers. She can't smell me from there.

I hang my red Cats sweatshirt next to my majorette uniform and my Foamy's outfit. I have forty sisters now. That's what they call us, though it's nothing like being sisters with Kayla. Still, I have forty new sisters. Mama and Daddy Dean lie clean and loving in their beds. The bathroom beacon shines welcome into the darkness.

I wonder why I feel so alone.

Chapter 11

The Monday after initiation, Mr. Page hands back my Algebra test. At the top corner of the paper I find a red A, with a small plus sign after it. "Nice work—again," he wrote. But he knows Math isn't work to me. It's a game I enjoy playing. A treat I give myself like some people give themselves a good book to read. Algebra is a logical system. It might be challenging, but it doesn't trick you. I wish life were more that way. If I didn't have so many other important things to do, I would spend more time preparing for this, my favorite class.

Mr. Page knows Daddy Dean through the Wilma Lions Club. Lately, he's been asking "How is he today, on a scale of 1 to 10?" I appreciate his giving me a quick way to report on Daddy Dean's condition. Today, I answer "4"— Daddy Dean seemed withdrawn this morning, below average. Average now is not what it used to be. Before, it would have meant up and about, puttering, joking. Now it means in bed, but eating some and able to visit in the afternoons.

"Four," says Mr. Page, thoughtfully. "And how about you?"

"Okay," I answer. I can never gauge myself on a scale of 1 to 10.

When the bell rings, Mr. Page begins a review of Sets and Real Numbers for those who didn't do well on the test.

Connie Frost catches my eye. Her smile is bright, her clothes are bright, her jewelry is bright. She looks a lot different than she did Saturday night at initiation. She gives me the Cat signal. I curl my fingers and return the signal under my desk. I have to. Club rules.

Mr. Page looks from me to Connie, then up at the ceiling. He knows all about the Cats and the KOs, but I don't think we make much sense to him. I'm feeling better about the Cats today. The older members are really acting friendly, trying to make up for what they put us through, I guess. Now that it's over, I'm glad I'm in. Still, I wish Mr. Page hadn't seen me give Connie the claw.

The intercom crackles, diverting his attention.

"Mr. Page?"

"Yes?" He sounds irritated. We all know how he hates to be interrupted by what he calls the "faceless voice."

"Please send Wray Jean Child to Mr. Sharp's office."

I'm confused. I never schedule meetings during Algebra. I can't think of why they would be calling me now. Unless . . .

Mr. Page must be thinking the same "unless . . ." because he stammers, "Wray Jean, would you, um, like someone to, uh, go with you?"

Oh, Jesus, I pray. No. I look around the room.

The kids are all staring at me, making me more afraid. Would I like someone to go with me? I shake my head. I don't trust myself to speak. I try to look casual, as if I have no idea why I am being called out of class.

On my way to Mr. Sharp's, I can't think, except for begging: Jesus, Jesus, oh please, no. I stand outside the School Activities Office. Don't be silly, I snap to myself, but my stomach doesn't hear me. It jumps and lurches at my speculations.

Mr. Sharp looks somber. "Sit down," he says. I read the plaque behind his desk: When the Going Gets Tough, the Tough Get Going. I click a mental picture of that plaque. For some reason, I want to remember everything about this moment, so that later I will be able to say—the day they told me, I sat in the Student Activities Office with the lights reflecting off the rims of Mr. Sharp's glasses. His paper clips glittered in their metal container. His pen glinted as he turned it over and over in his hands. His watch beamed a wavering streak across the ceiling. The black school clock hands pointed to 10:56. Mr. Sharp put his fingers together and said:

"I'm sorry to have to do this, Wray Jean, but I know you can handle it."

Don't cry, don't cry, don't cry.

"I'm sure you have an idea why I called you in this morning."

"Mmm-hmmm." My lips are tight. His are tighter.

"This is serious."

"Yes," I whisper. Daddy, Daddy. Jesus, Daddy Dean.

"You know, and I know," Mr. Sharp leans forward, "that clubs are forbidden."

I hold myself perfectly still, waiting for him to speak in English again. And then it sinks in. Clubs. So that's what this is about! Thank you, God, thank you, thank you. I unclench my hands and try to follow the rest of what Mr. Sharp is saying.

". . . strictly out of bounds," he drones. "I do not, will not sanction them. I would hate to have to reconsider your worthiness for School Leadership Council. I know you'll make the right choice."

I take a deep shaky breath, and another, before I am able to answer. "Yes, sir," I say. "And thank you!"

Now he's the one acting confused. "You're quite welcome," he says, guardedly. His face softens as I get up to leave. "By the way, I hear your father's been ill."

His noticing surprises me.

"I am a father myself," he begins in a kind and confidential tone. "I don't think yours would like that short skirt."

I look down at my knees.

"School leaders dress appropriately," he reminds me.

I want to skip out of his office, short skirt and all. Daddy Dean is fine, or Mama would have called. Silly me.

Algebra is over by the time I get back to class. The other students are gone. Mr. Page is waiting by the blackboard.

"Everything, um, okay?" he asks, afraid of the answer, I think.

"Yes!" I say.

"Good news?"

"Yes!" I walk over to the blackboard and pick up a piece of chalk.

A = the set of Cat members, I write.

n(A) = 41.

B = the set of SLC members.

n(B) = 55.

Mr. Page interprets. "There are 41 members in the Cats club and 55 members of Student Leadership Council."

Wray Jean ∈ A

"Wray Jean is a member of A."

Wray Jean ∈ B.

"Okay . . ."

n(A ∩ B) = 7

"Seven students belong to both A and B, the Cats and SLC."

I nod. This is fun.

Sharp's Laws, I write.

1.) { x/x is a Cat and a School Leader } = { 0 }

Mr. Page hesitates. "X such that x is a Cat *and* a School Leader is the empty set?"

"According to Sharp," I say.

∴, therefore

Wray Jean = 0

Mr. Page crosses his arms and waits.

I print out the second of Sharp's Laws.

2.) Wray Jean ∈ B if Wray Jean ∉ A

"Wray Jean is a member of B if and only if Wray Jean is not a member of A. Ahhh. Wray

Jean can belong to SLC if and only if Wray Jean does not belong to the Cats." Mr. Page's face lights up.

This is what teachers must see when their students learn something new, I think.

But then Mr. Page says, "You're on shaky mathematical ground, here, kiddo."

"Shaky ground, period," I joke. I write out Sharp's Third Law.

3.) $A \not\subset B$

"A is not a proper subset of B," I explain. "In other words, Cats are not a proper subset of SLC."

"Sharp's Third Law is algebraically correct," Mr. Page says, "but Wray Jean does *not* equal zero."

"Thanks," I say. I'm late for history, but I know Mr. Page will write me an excuse. I draw a number line from 1 to 10 and circle the four. I don't wish for Daddy Dean to be any higher on the scale. Right now I'm just happy he isn't any lower.

Mr. Page puts his arm around me and gives my shoulder a squeeze. I can't help grinning as he takes my chalk.

Wray Jean = 1,000,000, he writes.

It isn't logical at all. Mr. Sharp is threatening to kick me out of SLC. Daddy Dean's condition is below average. But in Math, and in the real world, everything is relative. Mr. Page is correct. I feel like a million.

Chapter 12

I spend extra time with Daddy Dean on Monday, Tuesday and Wednesday. He seems to be improving. When I open his door on Thursday, he acts more like a "6" than a "4."

"Come in," he says in a very eager, very alive voice.

I pull my chair close and sit, snug in the safe shadows. As my eyes adjust to the semidarkness, I notice his expression. I gather Daddy Dean has something special to talk about today.

"What do you want to be?" he asks.

I think I know the answer to that question. I want to be cuter and smarter. I want to have it all, to be a school leader and a Cat. Both. I want to be liked by everybody. I want to be somebody else. I know these are not the things Daddy Dean wants to hear.

"I want to be happy," I say.

He shakes his head. "No, I mean, what do you want to *do?* Later on. When you're . . . older."

I guess he means I can't be a majorette all my life. Or a carhop.

"Would you like to be a nurse or a teacher or a nuclear physicist? Maybe a carpenter," he suggests.

I giggle, but Daddy Dean is serious.

"I haven't really thought about it," I say.

"Do me a favor, would you? Think about it."

"What do *you* want me to be, Daddy Dean?"

He shakes his head again. "It doesn't matter what I want, understand? I want what you want. Just give it some thought."

He closes his eyes and opens his hand. I hold on while he falls asleep. His fingers relax after a while, but when I start to pull away, they tighten again. My hand is warm in Daddy Dean's. I sit beside him as he sleeps, and wonder what in the world he wants me to do.

When he wakes, his eyes are bright. "You're right," he says, out of the blue.

"About what?"

"About what you want to be."

"What's that, Daddy Dean?" I ask.

"Happy," he answers.

"Well, that sounds a lot easier than nuclear physics," I say.

He chuckles. "Be happy," he says.

He has closed his eyes again but I am pleased to see that I have made him smile. He squeezes my hand one last time, before I leave.

"Be happy." What is happiness? I wonder. I'll be happy when things are back to normal, when Daddy Dean is out of bed, when Mama gets her color back.

Chapter 13

I find Mama downstairs, ironing. The washing machine and dryer thrum together in the warm utility room.

Mama folds the pillowcases, patting each one as she stacks it on the end of the ironing board. The lighting is bad down here. Daddy Dean was always going to put in a better fixture. When things are back to normal, I bet that'll be on Mama's list of chores for him. First on my list will be finishing the bookcase. Together.

Somehow, in this bare-bulbed utility room light, the crisp white cotton fabric emphasizes Mama's washed-out skin. Everything about her is pale—pale brown hair, pale restless fingers, straightening out the edges, tidying the corners, smoothing, smoothing all the time.

Mama grabs a sheet from the laundry basket. She picks up the iron and pushes the steam button. The iron sighs. She rubs the hot metal over the material. Sighhhh. Extra pressure on a stubborn wrinkle. Sighhhh. Sighhhh. She takes a deep breath and slowly lets the air out through her nose. Sighhhh. The iron gurgles. It needs water.

"Mama, are you okay?" I ask.

She looks up and when she does, she presses a

65

big fold into Daddy Dean's sheet. She sets the iron upright and flops into a nearby chair. "I'm okay," she answers. "Just a little tired. Really. I'm fine."

What I hear doesn't fit with what I see. I am reminded of those "find ten things wrong with this picture" puzzles: gray circles under bloodshot eyes, sagging face, hollow voice, trembling lips. If I look hard enough, I can find all ten. But I don't want to see the contradictions to her words.

"You want me to stay home tonight and help?" I ask. "I'll be glad to. Someone can take my place at work. Bud and Arlene will understand."

"No, honey. Thanks. You need to get out. I'll be fine, just fine."

. . . creases etched into her forehead, eyelids at half-mast, shoulders sloped in a chronic droop . . .

I want to believe her so badly.

"Hey, Mama, did I tell you what Mr. Sharp did Monday?" This might cheer her up, I think, or at least get her mind off how tired she is. I repeat his big lecture on outside clubs and short skirts. I tell her about Mr. Page and me. I explain to her how glad I was, that it wasn't bad news about Daddy Dean. "Mr. Sharp just about scared the socks off me, calling me in like that," I tell her.

As I talk, I watch Mama's face turn angry, sad, and tired again. When I am finished, she looks the same as when I began. Except . . . something in her expression seems to warn me. I hesitate.

"I know it sounds dumb," I say, "but for a while there, I thought, I thought . . ." I pause, weighing whether or not to continue. "For a while there," I say, more firmly, "I thought he was

66

going to *die.*" I shake my head and shrug a wasn't-that-silly shrug.

Mama doesn't answer, but a startling blush of color springs into her face. Even under the bad light, I can see the flood of warm blood.

I feel my own blood pulsing at my temples. Say it was silly, I plead silently. It's hard to breathe in this room, under this harsh light. It's hard to think here.

"Honey . . ." Mama begins. She straightens her shoulders and looks me in the eye.

I need to go, to get away from her looking at me like that, to get out from under the glare of the utility room light bulb.

"Poe is picking me up for work pretty soon." I'll say anything to keep her from talking.

Mama sags backward into her chair. She rubs her eyelids with her fingertips.

"Mama?" I ask.

"Go," she says, softly. "You'll be late."

I wait for Poe by the door outside Daddy Dean's bedroom. I listen to his deep-sleep breathing. In. Out. I think of Mama blushing. Her reaction is a riddle. What was that all about? I wonder, pretending not to know. The answer threatens to surface. But my mind jumps back as if at something hot, something much more dangerous than a pale burning cheek.

Chapter 14

The evening of Thursday, October 24 will surely go down in Foamy's history as the slowest ever. The parking lot is deserted. Poe and I pack large tins of mustard and ketchup into cardboard boxes. Bud and Arlene will serve the dwindling crowds through November. That will be the end of the drive-in season until spring.

Arlene is wearing her new wig. I guess Bud always wanted to date a blonde, too. Blonde is better than red on Arlene, though I still like her natural color, black, best of all.

But the wig puts her in a playful mood. "I'm sending you girls home early, as soon as Bud and I get back from our dancing lessons. We'll close up after you leave." She moves towards the kitchen, "Are you ready yet, Lover Boy?"

"Ready as I'll ever be, Blondie." Bud whistles a little jingle and grabs Arlene by the waist. He twirls her around, then offers his arm. They look so happy together, it makes me want to cry.

"Good night, ladies," Bud sings.

"Don't eat all the profits." Arlene's not kidding.

When the door closes behind them it is suddenly

quiet inside the drive-in. Poe turns the volume up on the radio.

"Welcome to K-HIT, 760 on your dial," the announcer shouts.

"I can't stand it any longer," Poe says. "It's been almost a week. Tell me about initiation."

"The Cats have been sworn to secrecy," I say, in a stage whisper. "How about the KOs?"

"Oh, we have too! Should I go first?"

I nod. "I'll fix treats."

"Make mine a triple scooper." Poe settles herself on Arlene's stool. "Well, first of all, we had to dress like absolute ninnies—long underwear, hair nets, tennis shoes. We all met in Beverly Benson's basement."

"You didn't go to the park?"

"No, it was cold that night. Don't you remember?"

I remember all right. "Didn't you have to wear an onion around your neck."

Poe looks puzzled, then stern. "Quit interrupting," she orders.

"Sorry. Go on, go on."

"Then we get this big speech about how initiation is supposed to bring us all closer together."

I've heard that one, too.

"Then they drape these sheets over us, like togas."

"Whipped cream?" I ask.

Poe nods eagerly. I squirt a squiggle around the inside edge of her bowl.

"You can't tell anyone I told you this," she

69

says, when I hand her the mound of ice cream, covered with sauces and nuts and sprinkles.

"I won't. Promise." I start to work on my own sundae—ice cream and hot fudge and lots of each.

"Anyway, we go into this family room, and on the floor is a big low table with pillows all around it. There's a ton of food on the table—a huge pot of spaghetti noodles and another of sauce and clusters of grapes and bananas."

I cringe. I don't even like thinking about bananas. I foresee what Poe is going to tell me: that they were blindfolded, that they had to stick their hands in the noodles and were told they were intestines, that they had to pick up the grapes and were told they were eyeballs, strictly bush-league Halloween-type stuff, that they had to eat the bananas and were told they were . . .

"And get this!" Poe says.

"They blindfolded you, right?" I wonder if the KOs are really that smart, if they let the new members see the stuff before they put their hands in it. Not knowing for certain is what makes it so creepy.

"Not blindfolds. Cardboard tubes. Elbow restraints, so we couldn't bend our arms. Then they told us we had forty-five minutes to eat all the food, and that it had better be gone by the time they came back. Then they shut the door and left us. We all started grabbing for the food, but of course, we couldn't get it to our mouths because we couldn't bend our arms."

"So what did you do?" I twirl a ribbon of warm fudge around my plastic spoon.

"Well, Patti Summers had heard about this

70

same kind of thing at her church once. See, in Hell the people starved because they were so stinking selfish. They spent all their time figuring out how to feed themselves. But in heaven they fed each other. Get it? So we fed each other. I think that's what the KOs had in mind all the time. The spaghetti was hard to do but the sauce was almost impossible! It was really messy, but kind of fun, in a weird way. Pretty bizarre, huh?''

I feel sort of queasy. You don't know bizarre, I want to say. "So that was it?"

"Yeah. And they were right. We did feel closer afterwards.''

I watch my ice cream puddle into the bottom of the bowl. I think of something Uncle Raymond said once about life being a series of choices. "Even not choosing is a choice,'' he said.

I don't hate being a Cat. But after listening to Poe, I'm convinced the KOs are more my style. I guess, inside, I knew it all along. I'm beginning to wonder about my choices. They always seem so right at the time. Right and logical and good.

Poe digs into her triple scooper. "Well, come on,'' she says, between bites. "How about yours? I heard it was pretty bad.''

I take my bowl to the sink and rinse it, so I don't have to face her. "Well, you know, it was pretty much like yours.''

Poe doesn't answer. When I turn around, she is looking at me skeptically.

"Except,'' I say, as though I'm being painfully honest, as though I'm letting her in on some dark Cat secret, "except we got a little carried away with the food.''

71

"Bull!" Poe says, her mouth full of caramel sauce.

"What?"

"Bull Burnett, outside. Waiting." Poe swallows. She licks a speck of whipped cream from her lip. "How do I look?" she asks.

I'm checking out the blue station wagon with the blinking lights. "Fine," I say, automatically. I start to put on my sweater, but Poe is already headed out the door—eager, it seems, to be of service.

Bill Burnett is one of only three customers the whole night. We sell a double cheeseburger, a chili dog and a quart of root beer, though Poe and I can't figure out why anyone would want cold root beer in weather like this.

We have plenty of free time. "How's Daddy Dean?" Poe asks. "How is he, really?" And it's funny, but now that there's finally someone willing to listen, I don't feel like talking. So we gossip instead, and crank up the radio and dance in front of the milkshake maker.

Bud and Arlene get back at 9:45. It's only 10:00 when Arlene tells us to "scram."

Poe turns the heater on in her car. "It's been so great, catching up," she says. "I hate to stop now. You wanna go for coffee?"

"Sure why not?" I say. It isn't that late, after all. I might nod off at school tomorrow. But big deal. What will one cup of coffee hurt? In the whole scheme of things, what will one little cup of coffee matter?

We go to McGee's, the all-night pancake house downtown. One cup pours into three. An hour later, giggling and singing our club songs, we pull into my driveway.

"The light's out," Poe says.

That's the first thing I notice, too. The porch lamp is on, but the bathroom beacon has gone dark.

I stumble once, racing up the front steps. Inside, Mama is sitting at the kitchen table over her own cup of coffee.

"How's Daddy Dean?" I ask casually, trying to cover up my breathlessness.

She raises her head slowly. "He's gone," she tells me, in a deep, unfamiliar voice. Her words rumble over me like the roll of a kettle drum.

"Gone?" I whisper, my voice a flute, my voice a piccolo. "Where?"

Chapter 15

My bed feels secure and warm. I wake slowly, blinking, stretching. I yawn and turn to the clock. Bright hands glow in the darkness. Five-thirty. Too early to get up.

I nestle against the pillow once more, hoping for sleep. But something wants to make itself known to me. Something is crawling up through my muffled consciousness, pushing and pushing until it reaches me.

Daddy Dean is gone.

That explains the empty aching, filling me as reality oozes in. That explains the voices drifting in from the kitchen. Kayla flew home four days ago, the morning after Daddy Dean died. "I didn't get to say good-bye," was the first thing she said to me. "I should have been here," was my answer. "What could you have done?" she asked. "How could you have known?" I said. "Don't feel guilty," is what we've been trying to tell each other these past four days.

I slide out of bed and into my bathrobe. By the dim light of my bedside lamp, I examine myself in the mirror over the dresser. My eyes are puffy. I cried again last night, into the pillow so Mama wouldn't hear.

I walk through the dark living room, past the outlines of flowers sent by friends and relatives. The kitchen door is closed. I hear Mama telling Kayla about her call to Uncle Raymond. "He took it badly," she is saying. "I wish I hadn't told him."

I wish you hadn't needed to, I think.

When I open the door, two white faces turn in my direction.

"You're up?" Mama stubs out her cigarette and pushes herself from the table, making room for me to give her a quick awkward hug. Her ashtray overflows with cigarette butts. I wonder if she has been awake all night. She gestures toward the counter.

"Coffee's made," she says.

Two of Uncle Raymond's mugs sit by the pot. Mama has been falling into her old habits ever since Kayla's come home. WRAY JEAN, I read. DEAN.

I run my finger around the lip of Daddy Dean's mug. I fill the other and carry it to the table.

My chair scrapes across the floor. The sound grates against the stillness. I'm sorry, I want to say, sorry for making it worse. But how could it be worse?

Mama is watching me. She catches herself staring, jerks her eyes away, reaches automatically for the cigarettes. Only one is left in the pack. She has to dig for it. Then she puts it in her mouth and waits for Daddy Dean. The old routine. I haven't seen her do this for months. She goes for the matchbook, remembering he won't light it and then—I see it in her eyes—remembers he *can't*. I look away. How many times will it take, I wonder.

My sister sees it, too. Kayla, who hates the smoking, plucks the matches from the table. Kayla, who spouts words like emphysema and cardio-pulmonary disease, who says she doesn't understand why anyone would smoke, strikes the matchhead across the cover and raises the flame until it meets the end of the cigarette. Mama inhales. The paper ignites and the brown tobacco turns quickly to gray ash. Mama blows out a small cloud. She smiles at Kayla. It is a grateful, apologetic smile. Kayla snaps her wrist and drops the match into the ashtray. Nice going, Sis, I want to say. I touch her with my foot instead. She presses back. We agree, then. Today is not a day for quoting statistics.

Except for the methodical raising and lowering of her cigarette, Mama's hands are quiet. After all those weeks of scrubbing, fixing, straightening, smoothing and soothing, her hands are at rest.

We sit in the kitchen while the darkness lifts. It is a gray dawn, a black-and-white photograph of a morning. Mama suggests we all get showered and dressed.

"People will come by," she says. "They do that. They come by and bring food, the day of the funeral."

Chapter 16

People do come by. They bring hams and fruit breads and cheesy smelling casseroles for after the funeral. A few women from Mama's church group bustle about our kitchen, happy to be useful. The men seem less sure of themselves. Dr. Peck came by earlier to offer Mama a mild sedative. When she refused it, he built a fire in the fireplace, for something to do. Reverend Elliot is in the living room with Mama now, going over last-minute plans.

Dr. Peck follows me into the kitchen. He sits beside me at the table. When I look at him, I think, "You were here every day. Why didn't you do something?"

"We did everything we could," he tells me, as though he can read my mind. "It spread too quickly. We couldn't operate. Chemotherapy would have just made his last days miserable."

"Don't blame yourself" is what Mama told him. "Don't blame yourself. You did all you could."

But it wasn't enough.

Dr. Peck reaches out to pat my hand. I pull it away and fold my arms across my chest. I don't have Mama's capacity for forgiveness. Dr. Peck looks down at his own hand stretched out across the table. He slowly brings it back, runs his fingers through his hair, stands, goes to the coffee pot.

I pretend not to hear the whispers around me. "It's a blessing, really, that he went so fast, not much pain, got to stay at home." Reverend Elliot tries to comfort me before going back to the church for the funeral. "God has a plan for us all," he says.

Dr. Peck heaves a sigh. He reaches into the cupboard. He knows our house by now. He has been here enough times, administering what knowledge and medication he could. Suddenly, he throws his head back. His face crumples. He is hurting, I think, watching his eyebrows twist. I stand to get a better look and see him holding Daddy Dean's mug.

In a second I am beside him. I take the mug, touching him in the process, letting my hand linger on the clean narrow fingers that couldn't save my father. "It's okay, Dr. Peck," I say softly. "I'll get you another one." I pour his coffee and leave him to the bustling women.

I carry Daddy Dean's mug to my room. I kiss the place where his lips have been. I hide the mug in my dresser, where it will be safe among the folds of my sweaters.

I stay in my room until the outsiders are gone, and the house is ours once more. Then I settle myself by the fireplace in the empty living room. I don't really expect the small flames to warm the place where I am coldest.

Cards and letters have been filling our mailbox

for the past couple of days. They tell me what I already know—that my father was a good man, a decent man, with many friends. Most of the letters are to the whole family, but today there are several addressed in my name. I pull my chair closer to the fire and throw on a few sticks of cedar to get it blazing again. Then I read the kind words meant just for me.

Bud and Arlene have sent a flowery message, not like they really talk at all. Mr. Sharp's card has a picture of a pond on the front and a poem of sympathy inside. There is one from Leeza Sutter that says, "I don't know what to say. We're all so sorry. I wish I knew what to say, but I don't. Love, Leeza and the Cats." Mr. Page wrote, "Sometimes the numbers don't add up. My thoughts are with you."

People are good. They do their best. That's what Mama says.

The last note is on a folded piece of notebook paper. I open it and read two hastily written sentences: "Death has not captured your father. I've seen him!" The letter chills me, in spite of the fire. There is no signature. The note looks like something a kid would write. Someone from school, maybe?

I reread the words. They are like something out of my dreams. Because, in my sleep, Daddy Dean comes to me. He looks like he did a year ago— healthy and smiling. We talk. We pound nails. We eat elephant-shaped pancakes. But these are dreams. Right now, I am painfully awake. I hide the words in the pocket of my funeral-going dress. I wonder why someone would write them.

Not all people are good. Not all people do their best.

Some are cruel and some are cranks and some are just plain crazy. I guess I have a pretty good idea who wrote the letter, now that I think about it. I don't need to check the return address to find which city it came from. I throw the envelope in the fire and watch it curl into a sheet of ash. Only then do I dare hope I'm wrong.

I move restlessly to the front window. A shiny black limousine snakes its way down our street, sneaking up on our house as I imagine the ambulance did last Thursday night—no lights, no siren, no need to hurry. Quiet as a cat burglar, stealing my father away.

The limo frightens me. I thought we would go in our own car. Mama comes out of the little guest room wearing her dark blue suit. In the mirror over the fireplace, she applies her lipstick in two fluid movements. "He would want us to be brave," she says. "He would want us to be strong." I want to be like Mama today. Strong and brave, after all she's been through. But Kayla has to push me out the door, and once in the church, she has to nudge me up the steps to the balcony, where we watch Daddy Dean's friends and acquaintances fill the pews.

I don't notice the casket until Reverend Elliot stands beside it. Mama has chosen a bronze-colored one. Fall flowers cover the top. "Is he . . ." I ask Kayla, "is he . . . in . . . there?" She nods, holding a handkerchief to her face, blinking back tears in her attempt to be strong and brave.

But Reverend Elliot says, "Dean Child is not in this casket. He is in a better place. And he isn't suffering anymore."

Mama's words exactly. "He isn't suffering anymore," she told me the night he died. "You wouldn't want him to suffer, would you?" I reach into my pocket for a tissue. I touch the letter. Yes, I think desperately, I could want him to suffer, if it meant my father weren't really dead, if it meant I could see him again.

I listen to people singing his favorite hymns, telling stories about him, remembering his humor.

His friends carry the casket away. I don't see it again until the cemetery, where it is lowered slowly into a deep rectangular hole. Reverend Elliot leads us in prayer. The pallbearers unpin the white carnations from their lapels and drop them on the top.

Mama and Kayla and I grasp hands, gripping and clinging to each other for bravery, for strength. The air is filled with our silent sadness. I think of Daddy Dean's hand, reaching out.

And I beg, "Nonononono! Don't go, Daddy Dean. Come back! Please, God, oh please, please, come back."

And Kayla shakes with rough, uncontrollable sobs joined by long wordless wailings.

And Mama weeps. "Why oh why we did everything we could I never thought this would happen to you to me to us I love you."

The other mourners stare at the ground. No one looks our way, as the bronze casket sinks into the earth. Because on the outside, we are just three grim quiet figures, holding hands.

Chapter 17

Poe's folks have invited us for Thanksgiving dinner. I offer to do the shopping for Mama's cranberry-nut jello mold.

I drive to the grocery. Daddy Dean's car passes me going the other way. I whip my head around to see him. I start to wave, but he is too far down the road. I shake my head. It couldn't be.

I begin creating possibilities. *Maybe Daddy Dean went out of the country for illegal treatments. He didn't want to get our hopes up, so he just pretended to be dead. Now he's back in Wilma, driving his blue Ford.* Wait a minute. *I'm driving Daddy Dean's car.* I pull into the parking lot and rest my head against the steering wheel until I can breathe normally again.

This keeps happening. I see cars like his, faces like his, a familiar gesture. Then off I go, imagining. *He went to the hospital that night and the doctors were able to remove all the cancer, but the operation left him so crippled and hideous-looking, he couldn't face us again. He's alive somewhere. Isn't it possible?* No, I know it's not. *But maybe the government sent him on a dangerous mission in exchange for top-secret cancer treatments. He'll be back. He'll come walking up our front steps one of these days. Maybe, maybe.* Not a chance.

I buy Mama her walnuts, her boxes of strawberry jello and a bag of fresh whole cranberries. In the check-out line, the man behind me tells his daughter to get more sweet potatoes. "I'm so hungry, I could eat a horse," he says. And it starts all over again.

When I get home, I watch Mama chop the nuts. Kayla is dissolving jello in boiling water.

"I'm not feeling very thankful," I say.

Kayla nods.

Mama stops chopping. "I am," she says. "I had twenty-five good years with your father. I wouldn't trade them for anything."

"But was it worth it?" Kayla asks. I know what she's getting at. If Mama hadn't had all those good years with Daddy Dean, she wouldn't be hurting so badly right now.

Mama scoops the nuts into a glass bowl. "It would have been worth it if we'd had only two years. You really can't weigh these things against one another."

Mama sounds like she really means it, but I don't believe her. The longer you care about someone, the more you miss him after he's gone. That's what makes sense to me.

When Rusty drives into our driveway the day after Thanksgiving, I'm waiting for him on the front porch.

"I have something to tell you," I say.

He smiles up at me from two steps below. "Shoot," he says cheerfully.

"I don't want to see you for a while."

The look on Rusty's face makes me want to crawl under a rock. It's the same look he gets when he's been thrown. One second he's in the saddle and the next, he's on the ground, bruised and surprised. That's how he looks now.

"Why?" he asks, though he doesn't need to. His whole face shouts the question.

I give him the only answer he can't argue with. "Because I don't like you anymore."

He seems small, two steps down. When he stuffs his hands in his pockets, his shoulders hunch over, making him smaller yet. "Okay," he says softly. He squints up at me. I'm afraid he's trying to read my mind. I hold my mouth in a firm line. "Okay," he says again. "Bye."

He walks away on those crookedy legs of his. He pulls his keys from his pocket and shakes them in the air. Then he turns slowly and heads back toward the house. "You been talking to your Uncle Raymond again?" he asks.

"No," I answer, defensively. "What does he have to do with it?"

"*You* know. Uncle Raymond. Big dreams. All those clever sayings." Rusty rests his boot on the porch step.

Hurry up and go, I want to say. But I don't. "I still don't get it," I tell him.

"I think *I* do." Rusty lifts himself to the first step and plants a boot on the second. "You're always telling me about those clever sayings. How about this one: Never love, never lose. You heard that one before? Or did you just make it up yourself?"

Rusty is standing beside me now and I'm the one looking up.

I start crying because he makes me so mad, refusing to believe what I tell him. Stubborn old thick-skulled farmer boy.

"I hate you!" I say.

He cups his hand around my neck and draws my head to his chest.

"I hate you!" I don't fight him because the longer I fight, the longer he'll stay. Pretty soon, he'll get tired of holding me and patting my back and stroking my hair. He'll go and I'll be glad. Bowlegged rodeo bum.

"I hate you!" I feel Rusty's heart thumping hard and fast, the way hearts do after a close call.

"I love you, too," he whispers.

"I wish I had someone like Rusty." Poe and I are cruising Main Street on Saturday afternoon. She opens her thermos to pour me a cup of hot chocolate. I hold it in one hand while I steer with the other.

"Yeah," I say. "I guess it takes more than words to throw old Rusty."

Poe and I have spent a lot of time together since the funeral. Mostly, we drive and talk, for hours and hours, eating Halloween candy, or drinking hot cider from her thermos. Today, we nibble turkey sandwiches. She has listened to the saga of Daddy Dean's illness, everything I can remember from beginning to end. Now I've come to the part where I get the mysterious letter. I pass it to her and head out of town, toward Farmdale.

While Poe reads, I let my eyes wander over the

stubbled wheat fields. I hear her swear. "Who would write something like this?" she asks.

"I don't know," I lie.

"Some kook," Poe offers. "Some very sick person."

I don't like her answer any more than I like my own. "Listen," I say, "sometimes I think I've seen Daddy Dean." I tell her about the cars and the gestures and the faces. I tell her about my elaborate rationalizations of how he could still be alive. "Does that mean I'm a basket case, too?"

"Pull over." Poe sounds angry, her voice like the gravelly crunch of tires on the roadside.

I turn off the engine.

"We know what we know," she says firmly.

"Yes." I do know. Death has captured Daddy Dean. He won't be coming back.

"And if you think you're crazy, you're . . . crazy!" Poe says. "After my grandpa died, I saw people who reminded me of him all the time. I used to dream up ways he could still be alive, too. I think everybody does that. But I knew the truth. So do you. You're weird, Wray Jean. You're hopeless and you're too ambitious for your own good. But aside from trying to break up with Rusty, which, in my opinion, borders on insanity, I'd say you're definitely not nuts."

"Gee, thanks," I say. I hope my sarcasm covers my relief. I'm not nuts.

Weird, hopeless and ambitious, I can handle.

Chapter 18

I miss Kayla. She went back to college after Thanksgiving vacation. Mama misses her, too. I can tell. They were always close. They think alike, speak the same language. After Kayla left, Mama acted lost, but now she seems to have recovered her old energy. She's been cleaning out the closet and drawers in Daddy Dean's room. Me, I like having his things around. I like the look and feel and smell of them. I go into his room and lie on his bed, to be close. When Mama finds me, she says, "Come on out of there, Wray Jean. That's not good for you." It *is* good for me. But it's bad for her.

Kayla knows what bothers Mama. She would understand about the Goodwill Van, coming today to take the boxes by the front door.

"Someone ought to get some use out of them," Mama says of Daddy Dean's clothes.

She's right, of course. Daddy Dean doesn't need them anymore. His old workshirt is folded neatly on top a pile of give-aways. I pick it up, watching for Mama's reaction.

"Why do you want that old thing?" she asks. "It has paint spots all over it."

"I don't know," I say. Maybe I should choose something nicer. But this is what I want.

Kayla would pick something sensible, something Mama could understand. Mama has already given her Daddy Dean's keyring. And she has the heart-shaped necklace he bought for her seventeenth birthday.

I hang the shirt in my closet. I touch it as I get ready for school each day, until Christmas vacation finally arrives.

Kayla is wearing the necklace when she comes home for the holidays. I think it's her way of being close to Daddy Dean. She wears it when we bake sugar cookies and when we build a snowman in the backyard. She wears it now, as we sit by the fire with Mama, reading Christmas cards.

I wouldn't be doing any of these things. But Mama has said, "He would want us to enjoy the holidays." Would he? When I die, I'm going to have a section in my will that says: You have my permission to be miserable the first year. Skip the decorations and the stockings and the gatherings, if you want. And then people will say, "She wouldn't mind us feeling bad," and they won't have to pretend.

Still, it's nice to have Kayla back home, nice for the three of us to be together. We even laugh, once in a while, surprising ourselves.

Mama passes me a card. "Here's one from Raymond."

"You're kidding," Kayla says. "This I've gotta see."

Uncle Raymond hardly ever sends mail. He'd rather talk on the phone. "Person to person is my

88

style," he says. But he has sent a card with a jolly old St. Nick on the front. Inside, are the words to *The Night Before Christmas*. Printed below is the message: "May you laugh when you see him, in spite of yourself." Very fitting for us this year.

"Love, Uncle Raymond," he wrote beneath his perfect greeting. His careful, childish script seems familiar, though I rarely see it. I look at his signature for a long, long time. Then, like a sleepwalker, I carry the card to my room.

Kayla tags after me. "I want to see the card," she complains. "Where are you going? What's wrong?"

I take the letter from my desk. I hold it next to the card. Though one is neat and the other scribbled, the handwriting matches. "Are these the same?" I ask Kayla.

Her "yes" just confirms what I've known all along.

I tell her the whole story as we stare at the writing in front of us: Death has not captured your father. I've seen him!. . . . Love, Uncle Raymond.

"*Why?*" I don't expect Kayla to have an answer.

"Maybe Uncle Raymond can't tell the truth from what he wants the truth to be anymore," she says, gently.

That's exactly what Mama would do, make excuses for him. I'm bone tired of excuses. Didn't he know how much his letter would hurt me? I guess not. I guess he's just changed this year, at Hearthaven. His mind's gone soft and squishy, like a tangerine left too long in the toe of a

Christmas stocking—an improbable occurrence, but possible. "Anything is possible," he used to say. He always had all the answers. How could he let this happen?

"Don't show Mama," Kayla tells me. "It would break her heart."

What about my heart? I don't ask.

I take Daddy Dean's mug from my dresser. It reminds me of Hearthaven now. Kayla follows me to the kitchen. "We're going to make some cocoa," she tells Mama.

"That sounds wonderful," Mama is curled up in her blanket like a cocoon. Kayla knows what makes Mama happy and what makes Mama sad.

I push Daddy Dean's mug to the very back of the cupboard so I won't come across it by accident.

Kayla heats milk in a saucepan.

"I knew all along he wrote it," I tell her. "But I didn't want to admit it. I wanted to make it into this mysterious message with some hidden meaning instead of the ramblings of an old guy who doesn't have all his marbles." I'm ashamed of myself as soon as the words are out. I've made cracks about Uncle Raymond's "craziness" before. But they're not funny any more. Old guy. Lost his marbles.

Kayla nods. It's easy for her to agree. She never did take Uncle Raymond seriously. "Finding out is like a gift," she says. "You can let go now."

Let go of what? The letter? Uncle Raymond?

I watch her measure out the powdered cocoa, her necklace resting on her chest. A gift is a heart-shaped pendant, set in diamonds, hanging from a

90

gold chain. Discovering the truth about the letter is more like having the wind knocked out of me. Because the Uncle Raymond I thought I knew would never have done this.

If unwrapping the truth is such a gift, Kayla, then answer me this: Who will I believe in now?

There is no December FLAVR of the MONTH. The sign at Foamy's says Closed for the Season.

At home, Mama and Kayla decorate the tree while I sit by the window, remembering other Christmases. I watch the snow fall, coldness upon coldness. Mama hands me a silver ball to hang. I shake my head "no." I try to smile. She tries to smile back.

I used to stare into these shiny ornaments and laugh at my huge nose. Now I find the image accurate. The real me *is* distorted. And I am feeling fragile. If someone tried to touch me now, I mean, really touch me, I would break as easily as this glass globe, the shattered pieces reflecting broken bits of Christmas.

I wonder what will happen if I don't develop a hardness, a way of dealing with Daddy Dean's death and Uncle Raymond's decline. I think if I work at it, I can shut the door on my grief. I can pull the curtains on my memories and lock my feelings in a hidden place.

I think if I work at it, I can close myself for the season.

Chapter 19

I wake before the alarm can disturb the calm of my morning. I am in control.

One—I lay the covers back, two—plant my feet on the floor, three—stand, four—put my robe on, five, six, seven—step to my desk. Eight—sit.

Choreography. Perfected over these thirty-one days of January. The clock is my accompanist. The mechanical *ticka-ticka* keeps me counting.

I turn the switch on my desk lamp. The bulb hums as it lights up my calendar. I pencil a precise mark by today, a new day. Friday. The mark means "routine intact."

Next, I review my list of New Year's Resolutions. Today's tally shows I have earned nearly all my School Leadership Council points. Not surprising. I met with Mr. Sharp on Monday, January 6 at exactly 8:40 A.M. "If there's any job you want me to do, let me know," I told him. He was happy to oblige. I have been posting notices, typing file labels and folding brochures for PTA. I have also been ringing up points like an old-time pinball machine. "Or like a little robot," Poe grumbled the other day. Well, there are worse things to be, I guess.

Sometimes, I bring work home. "Don't stay up

too late," Mama tells me. I drink one cola per hour and get to bed by 2:00 A.M. I don't need much sleep anymore. Emotions make a person tired, not activity.

When I'm not doing projects for SLC, I study. Last night, I finished a paper on World War II. This morning, I check off New Year's Resolution #4—Extra Credit: History, Chemistry, Biology. I've learned something new; I don't have to like a subject to grind out a paper on it. I used to spend long evenings bent over equations, enjoying the "ahhh" feeling when I solved a particularly difficult problem. I knew if I worked it right, the answer would come eventually. It was fun, like connecting a big jigsaw puzzle. But I don't bother with Algebra anymore. I can ace the class without even trying.

I can ace these other classes, too, with enough extra credit. The teachers love it. They write me comments. They're so pleased I'm showing more interest. They're so happy I'm grasping the concepts. Blah, blah, blah. So what? Straight A's are just another goal, Resolution #5 on my New Year's list. I'm not interested in Mussolini or hydrocarbons or dead frog guts.

I'm interested in keeping busy. When there's nothing to do, I find myself drifting, remembering things I'd rather forget. And this morning, all these checked-off resolutions leave me with a panicky feeling. Wray Jean, I tell myself, you are in control. I pick up my pencil and add to the list. "More goals. See Mr. Sharp *today*."

On the way to the Student Activities office, I

pass John Zimmerman. "Hey, John," I say automatically.

He looks surprised. "Hey, Wray Jean," he answers.

Zimmerman, I think. I've finally matched every annual picture face to every student body member. When did I finish the Z's, I wonder. What does it mean, anyway? That I can cross off another goal. That my list is getting shorter.

All the more reason to see Mr. Sharp.

"Hello!" He stands—*stands*—when I enter his office. And to think I used to be afraid of him. He hasn't mentioned the Cats since that first lecture in October. I guess all my other activities make up for the fact I'm breaking Mr. Sharp's rules.

"What can I do for you?" he asks, sitting, motioning for me to sit, too.

"I have some spare time," I tell him, "at night."

"That amazes me," he says. He grins. I focus on the shiny whiteness of his teeth.

"So I was wondering," I continue slowly, "if you have anything . . ."

"Say no more!" Mr. Sharp pulls a canvas apron from his desk drawer. The Wolverine logo is stamped across the bib. "We need another ticket taker for the basketball games. The apron is yours afterwards—a bonus for all your hard work."

He grins again. I stare at his mouth while he tells me I have accomplished more in one month than most students do in one year. "Your father would be proud," he adds.

I shrug. I think not. I remember the day I tried to explain to Daddy Dean my three-year plan for

changing. It was the summer before my sopho-
more year and I wanted to share my vision of a
"new and improved" Wray Jean. We were sitting
in Mama's vegetable garden, about to sneak the
first of her cherry tomato crop. Daddy Dean kept
interrupting me. "Feel this," he'd say, scooping
up a handful of dirt. "Smell this," he'd say,
waving a tomato vine under my nose. "You're not
listening," I complained. He picked three small
perfect tomatoes. The way he held them, you
would have thought they were precious stones.
You would have thought Mama could grow rubies,
or something. I gave up trying to get through to
him. He offered me one of the little tomatoes.
"Taste this," he said. I bit into salty-sweet juicy-
warm ripe-red summer. I chewed slowly, wanting
the pure pleasure of it to last forever. Daddy Dean
watched me, close and careful. "Don't change too
much," he told me. "I kind of like you the way
you are."

As I reach for the Wolverine apron, I wonder
how Daddy Dean would like the little robot I've
become.

Mr. Sharp has mistaken my shrug and my
silence for signs of modesty. His teeth gleam.

"I wish we had more like you," he says.

Chapter 20

More like you—1,2. More like me—2,3. More, more—3,4—5,6,7,8.

Mr. Sharp's words mingle with the steps of a new majorette routine I'm working out. We're due to perform at a basketball game in March, less than a month away. I'm trying to live up to my responsibilities as head majorette, but the low ceiling of our living room is cramping my style. I wish the snow would melt, so I could work outside.

The year I turned nine, I practiced for my first Memorial Day parade in the wide open space of our backyard. Daddy Dean was painting the window trim. "That looks fun," he called from his ladder perch. "Let *me* try." So I gave him my extra baton and taught him the steps. We strutted around the yard together. I stretched my legs into high graceful kicks. Daddy Dean tried to keep up, looking comical in his baggy khakis and paint-speckled shirt. For our grand finale we tossed our batons so high in the air we stopped marching just to watch them come down. Then we both ran for cover. Just as the batons thudded to the ground, we heard the sound of clapping coming through the screen door. Mama and Kayla were watching from the kitchen window. Together, Daddy Dean and I took a bow.

Twirling was more fun then, outside on the grass.

I count out a difficult sequence that will end in a spectacular aerial toss. When the phone rings, I don't miss a beat. Mama is in the kitchen, resting her feet after a full day's work at the library. Though they're paying her now, she would do it for free. "It gives me a reason to get up in the morning," she says. But she moves slowly at night. It takes her five rings to answer the phone. I'm hoping it's Kayla.

"Raymond!" Mama squeals.

My baton flies across the room, bouncing off the wall and dropping behind the sofa. It's been weeks since we've heard from him. He hasn't answered Mama's calls, either. I was beginning to picture him straight-jacketed and silent, unable to hold the receiver, let alone converse. I climb over the sofa to retrieve my baton.

"Wray Jean," Mama calls. "Your Uncle Raymond's on the phone! He wants to talk to you!"

I drop to a crouch.

"I'll go get her," Mama says. Her footsteps pause at the doorway to the living room.

Does she see the gray dent in the wall, I wonder. How will I explain my hiding to her when I can't explain it to myself? In the old days, I would have jumped at the chance to talk to Uncle Raymond. But now I feel shy of him. I don't know how to respond to the new Uncle Raymond, the wounded one who hasn't been able

97

to turn adversity into advantage. I force myself to hold still until Mama is back on the phone saying, "She was here a minute ago. I guess she's gone out."

Then I crawl behind the end table, over the lamp cord and into the hall. I was the only one who couldn't see Uncle Raymond for what he really was—a sad, sorry man. He spent his whole life trying to be a success, then lost it all. That's what I heard him tell Mama and Daddy Dean. "There's nothing left. Nothing." What kind of hero is that?

I tiptoe to my room and curl up on the bed. Mama is always telling me to get more rest. She'll be delighted to find me napping before dinner.

I wait ten minutes before I hear her whisper.

"Wray Jean?"

I rub my eyes.

"I guess you were asleep when I called." Mama's voice has an excited edge to it. "Raymond phoned," she says, "after all these weeks! I think he's been using up his energy getting better."

It hurts me to hear Mama fooling herself.

"He's been selling his pottery through a shop in Raleigh. Isn't that great?"

Terrific, I think. From real estate whiz to clay pounder, by way of the looney bin. Good old Uncle Raymond. The thought has sprung to my mind, mean and ugly. I wonder why I suddenly feel so nasty toward him. Is it his fault he can't cope?

"Mama, how exactly did Uncle Raymond lose all his money?" I ask.

She looks confused. "Lose it?"

"He told you there was nothing left, right before he went . . . before he . . . *you* know."

Mama leans against my dresser. "Wray Jean, your Uncle Raymond is still a wealthy man, money-wise."

"He said he lost everything."

"He meant Elizabeth," Mama says, quietly.

Elizabeth, the fiancée? Uncle Raymond introduced us in Raleigh. I remember hoping that one day someone would say my name the way Uncle Raymond said hers.

Elizabeth. I always thought there was more to it than a broken romance.

Mama lifts her hand as if to wipe away my scowl. "We both know how it feels to lose someone we love," she says. "Raymond couldn't handle it. He needed help. Your father suggested Hearthaven. Raymond always admired your father. He says he was like his own brother, always willing to talk things out."

I'd rather not listen to Mama fill me in on any more of Uncle Raymond's warped ideas about Daddy Dean.

"If he's so rich, why work for a pottery shop?" I ask, to change the subject.

"Because he loves it! He hated real estate." Mama's voice sounds bitter. She clears her throat. "Raymond has always been creative," she says proudly.

"Don't feel bad about missing him," she adds as she leaves my room. "He wants to keep in better touch from now on. He says he's going to call regularly, on Thursday nights.'' Mama sounds so hopeful.

I know better. Most likely, it's another of his delusions. I'm sure he won't call again. But just in case, I fill in my calendar for the next three weeks. I've spent my whole life memorizing Uncle Raymond's silly mottos, only to find them meaningless. Now I can't trust anything he says. Best for me to avoid him, pretend he never existed, forget everything he ever told me.

Thursday, February 20, I write—dinner with Poe. Thursday, February 27—movie with Rusty. Thursday, March 6—twirl at basketball halftime.

Better safe than sorry, I tell myself.

Touché, Uncle Raymond.

Chapter 21

Thursday, March 13, I drive past Foamy's on the way to the basketball play-offs. Arlene and Bud have changed their reader board. "Go Wolverines" it says. FLAVR of the MONTH—a taste of victory. Rah, rah, I whisper. I'll be glad when they reopen next month.

Taking tickets isn't a bad job. I don't get any tips, but it gives me a chance to practice names while I earn points. After the first quarter, I join Rusty in the stands. He's sitting with Poe and Bill Burnett, who have been dating since Foamy's closed last December.

The gym is smelly with sweat and perfume, but Rusty's denim jacket is fresh from the outdoors. I rest my chin on his shoulder.

"Comfortable?" he asks.

I nod. I could doze off if I'd let myself.

Bill leans forward. "You two going to the dance?"

"What dance?" I ask.

"Basket!" Rusty shouts suddenly. "Nice going Murdock."

"The Spring Fling," Poe says. "Rusty, can't you guys come up with a better name?"

Rusty looks at her, distracted. "These are the

play-offs. You know, championship possibilities, trophies. . . ."

We stare back at him. He sighs and turns to me. "On behalf of the Future Farmers of America, I extend my invitation to the FFA Spring Fling."

"Yuk," says Poe.

"What's the rush, Cowboy?" I tease. "That dance is a month away."

Then I remember. Bill asked Poe the day after Christmas vacation.

"I'll have to wait and see if I get a better offer between now and then," I say lightly, feeling bad about embarrassing Bill. He and Poe aren't at the kidding stage yet.

"What's wrong," murmurs Rusty, "don't you like me any more? Again?" He's teasing back, but he's also reminding me that I am capable of hurting him. When I told him "I hate you," he answered "I love you, *too*." Amazing. How does a person know to do that? Somehow he figured out what I was going through and what I really meant. I would never have been so perceptive. I take things too literally. Not Rusty. He ignored my words then and he ignores them now.

"Yes, we're going," he tells Bill, "And no, we can't change the name," he tells Poe. "Now let's watch the game."

We turn our attention to the court. The halftime buzzer blares and the players head for the locker room.

Rusty groans. I shrug. I don't care much about the game, anyway. It just feels good to sit still for a while and rest.

"Shall we wake you when the game starts?" Poe asks.

I open my eyes to make a face at her.

The cheerleaders are led by Leeza Sutter, last year's Spring Fling Queen. They bounce onto the floor to do a dance routine with the squad from the Bombers team. Leeza glances nervously into the bleachers behind us, where Connie Frost sits with Animal Gates.

"You guys were better," Poe says.

The majorettes got a standing ovation at last week's halftime. I'm glad we're not performing tonight. I don't think I could march three steps.

"Let's double to the dance," Poe suggests.

I nod.

"Sounds good," Rusty says.

Bill blushes.

The gym warms up again after the start of the third quarter. The Wolverines edge ahead of the Bombers 67 to 64. But that's not the only game being played out to the squeak of tennis shoes and the bursts of pep band rally songs.

I watch Poe and Bill, heads together, discussing something private. Yayyyy, I think. Yayyy for Poe. Yayyy for Bill.

I hear Connie Frost's voice cut through the rest of the noise. "Oh, Eddie, isn't this exciting?" No one else calls Animal by his real name. It sounds like Connie is moving in on Animal. Foul, I think. Booooo, Connie. Boo, Animal. Isn't there a code of ethics about Cats dating the boyfriends of other Cats? Maybe I'm seeing things that don't exist. Like Uncle Raymond does. Connie's probably just keeping Animal company while Leeza's busy performing her back handsprings.

After the fourth quarter, I watch Connie and Animal join the cheerleaders. Connie drapes her arm over Leeza's shoulder. But her other hand keeps finding ways of touching Animal, brushing against his letter jacket, grazing his knuckles. Am I the only one to notice?

I try not to stare, concentrating instead on the crowd of people leaving the bleachers. I act cheerful and peppy, instead of grumpy and sleepy, the way I really feel. Acting has become second nature to me over the winter.

"Good game," Rusty says, on the way out.

I don't answer. I'm getting sick of games.

Chapter 22

"So tonight's the big fling," Poe says, off-handedly. She's excited about her first dance with Bill. If she really thought so little of it, she wouldn't have asked Arlene to help her pick out a dress pattern. She wouldn't have taken three weeks to sew herself a dusty-rose puff-sleeved gown. She wouldn't be sitting on my bed, painting her toenails passion pink.

I haven't decided what to wear. I still can't believe it's spring already. Where did winter go? A dark gray blur of meetings and extra credit projects. So much busyness. Mama all the time saying, "Don't overdo."

I stand before my closet, shaking my head. The dress I bought a month ago hangs on me like a gunnysack. I guess I've lost weight. And I can't very well wear my majorette uniform or my Foamy's outfit.

Poe kids me about my lack of planning. "I thought a School Leader was always prepared."

"No," I say, "you're thinking of the Boy Scouts."

I pull Daddy Dean's paint-spotted shirt off the hanger. I put it on over my slip. "Well?" I ask, twirling in a circle.

"Too damn short," Poe says, gruffly.

I laugh at her imitation. "But Daddy Dean," I whine in a high voice, "everyone is wearing shirts to the dance this year. I've just *got* to be in style."

"Over my dead body," Poe growls. "Oh, cripes. I'm sorry, Wray Jean. I can't believe I said that. I'm sorry. I'm sorry."

I shrug out of the shirt and hang it back up. "Don't be sorry," I tell her. "That's exactly what he would say. Then he'd say 'What's the matter with that long thing you used to wear at Christmas?' "

I find the green velvet skirt in the back of the closet, covered in plastic. I still have the blouse and shoes to match.

"What *is* the matter with it?" Poe asks, after I get it on.

"It's not too damn short," I say, easing up the zipper, "but it sure is too damn tight." I may have lost weight, but my waist is still bigger than it was in eighth grade.

"It looks fine to me," Poe says. "Can you breathe?"

"Barely."

I don't button the waistband until Bill pulls into the parking lot at school.

The gym has been transformed by the Wilma Chapter of the Future Farmers of America. "Everything looks great," I tell Rusty. I know he spent hours decorating today. Having the refreshment area set up like an outdoor café was his idea.

"You look great, too," he says.

"Liar." I know what I look like. Even make-up doesn't cover the dark circles under my eyes. But Rusty's just trying to be nice. I don't know why I've been snapping at him lately.

He points to a picnic table with an umbrella sticking out of it. "Shall we sit for a while?"

"No," I say, quickly. Sitting is the last thing I want to do in this skirt. "Let's dance."

Rusty likes the fast ones, the hard beat of the rock band, everyone bumping bodies under the flashing lights. But being jerked between light and dark is making me dizzy. I'm happy when the band plays a slow song. I love putting my head against Rusty's chest and swaying back and forth. Besides, I need to hold onto him for balance. Everything seems tilted somehow.

When the band takes a break, I try to excuse myself. If I can just get away and unbutton my waistband, maybe I'll feel better.

"Wait," Rusty says. "They're going to announce the Spring Court. Aren't you curious?"

"You can tell me about it when I get back," I gasp. Everything is closing in on me. I've worn snug clothing before, but I haven't ever felt like this.

"Don't leave now," Rusty wheedles. He won't let go of my hand. He smiles his sweet-Rusty smile, not knowing I'm beginning to rage inside. Not knowing I'd like to smack him one. Lighten up, I tell myself. It's not Rusty's fault. It's just the skirt—too damn tight. Squeezing me to death.

The princesses are no surprise. Patti Summers floats up to the stage, looking like an angel in her white ruffles. Connie Frost bounces brightly up the three stairs with Animal trailing behind her. Where is Leeza, I wonder. This is some sisterhood. Poe and I raise our eyebrows at each other. Poe would make a beautiful Spring Queen with her elegant gown and fine strong face. But there's not much chance of that. The same type of people get voted these things every time. I plan to make a break for it as soon as the announcer is finished.

"And this year's Future Farmers Fairest is . . . Miss Wray Jean Child, escorted by FFA member Rusty Hayes!"

Poe squeezes my hand and winks. Bill claps. They knew, I think. They've known all night. Rusty holds out his arm, formally.

"You have the manners of a southern gentleman," I tell him, ignoring my discomfort.

It's a long walk through the other dressed-up couples, past their corsages and smiles. Rusty guides me up the stairs to the stage. I stop in front of a folding chair draped with paper flowers and ribbon streamers. I say hi to Patti and turn to congratulate Connie, my sister Cat, already seated on her own decorated chair. She glances up at me, coldly.

I turn away, stung. Slowly her behavior becomes clear. If it weren't for me, she might be the Spring Queen. Then Animal would be placing a wreath of roses on her head as Rusty is doing now, to me.

He kisses my forehead. The time has come to settle gracefully onto my throne.

When I sit, my waistband cuts me off in the middle. I feel confined by my skirt, by everything going on around me. I risk another glance at Connie. Suddenly she smiles warmly. Her eyes crinkle, the Connie Frost trademark. A flashbulb explodes. And for all time, in the Wilma Wolverine annual, gracious Princess Connie will be smiling benevolently at the Future Farmers Fairest. And for all time, I will be caught in the Wolf Trap, confused-looking, my feelings hurt, my head pounding, my eyes blinded by the flash.

But I am the Spring Queen, one of the Wray Jeans I've always wanted to be.

I take a deep breath. My button pops.

I hear a nervous giggle. The joke's on me. Yes, funny. Sad-funny.

Connie's eyes widen. "What's wrong?" she demands, protective of her big moment.

Patti leans toward me. "Are you all right?"

She sounds so serious. Doesn't she see how funny it all is? Who's that laughing, anyway? Me? Howling, hysterical, ha, ha, ha. I look out over the gymnasium, full of people looking back. I know their faces. Annual picture faces. Little o's for mouths. Little surprised o's instead of smiles.

I don't care what they think. And I don't care that I don't care. And I don't care that I don't care that I don't care. . . .

Rusty's hands feel strong. Stick 'em up, I say. He pulls me gently out of my throne. Good boy. Good boy. Escort the Queen from her Court. Good-bye. Good-bye. Wave to your subjects, Wray Jean. Wave to Mr. Sharp. *Angry* Mr. Sharp.

Oops! Forgot the rules: School Leaders Don't Break Down.

Rusty's arm, tight around my shoulder, keeps me from flying apart. I close my eyes and sink against him.

My flower crown is slipping.

Chapter 23

"I told her not to overdo. Take it easy, I said. Get your rest." Mama stands behind Dr. Peck while he presses his fingers to my wrist. He seems out of place at my bedside, taking my pulse, feeling my forehead.

"Don't worry. She's fine," he tells Mama.

"A healthy girl does not leave the school dance in hysterics," she argues.

"She's exhausted, that's all. Overtired. Not enough sleep. Not eating right, most likely. Plus the stress of last fall."

No, not exhaustion, I want to say. Wrong, wrong.

"I should have insisted . . ." Mama begins.

Dr. Peck interrupts. "Don't blame yourself. Knowing Wray Jean, I doubt you could have prevented it."

Mama brushes my hair from my face. This has been her prediction all along: *You'll wear yourself out, Wray Jean.*

"Something else," I mutter, but it's too much of an effort to explain. I close my eyes instead, and when I open them, I am alone.

Dim light filtering through my curtains tells me it's still afternoon. Or did I sleep for a night and

a day? I have no way of knowing by the time—
4:15.

If I lie on my side, I can see past the clock into
my closet. The door is open. It was closed before,
when Dr. Peck examined me. Mama has hung my
long skirt. It seems odd to think of her moving
around in here, without my knowing it. So I guess
I did sleep right through. No, now I remember. I
ate soup for supper yesterday. Chicken noodle.
And crackers. The crumbs on my pillow are
scratching my cheek.

I concentrate on the closet.

Green, I think. Green. Brown. Beige. Blue and
white. Red.

My dance skirt hangs next to my Foamy's
outfit, next to my Wolverine apron, next to my
majorette uniform, next to my Cats sweatshirt.

All the Wray Jeans I wanted to be, lined up in
a tidy row.

I crawl out of bed to shut the door on the Spring
Queen, the Carhop, the School Leader, the Majorette, the Cat.

What am I without these scraps of fabric? I am
afraid to know. Afraid that without them, there is
no me. That there is nothing left. Nothing.

That's what I meant to tell Mama and Dr. Peck
yesterday. I meant to tell them their diagnosis was
wrong. It wasn't exhaustion that sent me into
hysterics at the dance. It was disappointment.

A paint-spotted shirttail hangs below the hem of
my majorette uniform. It reminds me of what
Daddy Dean told me to be. Happy.

But if being the Wray Jean I always wanted to
be doesn't make me happy, what will?

111

I slip the workshirt over my nightgown, and close the closet door. Then I make my bed, clean off my dresser, toss the wilted rose crown into the wastebasket. I turn my attention to the piles of books stacked on my floor. I'd like to put everything in order. I wonder where Daddy Dean kept the plans for my bookcase. I suppose I could just use bricks and boards.

Mama knocks softly.

"I'm awake," I say.

"So you are!" She doesn't seem to notice the workshirt. "Poe wants to visit as soon as you feel up to it," she says. "And Rusty sent these." Mama sets a small basket of primroses on my desk.

"Oh, and Mr. Sharp called. I explained about the dance and he says all is forgiven."

Just like him to assume a breakdown requires forgiveness, I think.

Mama frowns. "He asked me to remind you about the student body elections coming up at the end of April."

Ah, yes, I had forgotten about those.

"He wants you to run for Vice President, regardless of your demerits—whatever that means. He thinks you'd do a fine job. And even though you're short a few points, he'll allow you to make them up when you come back to school."

"He said demerits?" I ask.

Mama nods.

So all this time I *have* been losing points for being a Cat. What a crazy world! I start to giggle. Mama looks worried.

"It's okay," I tell her. "I can control myself."

"Well, it's up to you, of course, about the elections, but if you want my advice . . ." She clamps her lips together. "It's up to you."

Vice President is an important job at Wilma High School. Participating in Student Government was a big part of my three-year plan.

"I think I'll sleep on it," I tell Mama. The idea of student body elections makes me tired. I can figure out what to do with these books later.

Mama convinces me to eat a bowl of tomato soup. Then I sleep.

I wake before dawn, with an idea of where the bookcase plans might be. I button Daddy Dean's workshirt and wander through the house, my nightgown trailing behind me like a flower print ghost. I lift the hem as I go down the basement stairs.

I stop outside Daddy Dean's workshop, not sure what I'll find inside.

I push the door open. When I snap on the light, it shines yellow warm over cans of paint and turpentine, and tools hanging from their pegboard hangers. Just the way Daddy Dean left them. Even the sawhorses are up, ready and waiting.

My bare feet shrink from the cold of the cement floor. I step lightly, jerking back as one foot lands on the sharp corner of a large woodchip. I bend to pick it up. It reminds me of Daddy Dean sawing two-by-fours for the patio deck. It reminds me of pounding nails together. "Good job," I hear him say. I can almost feel his hand on my shoulder.

I put the woodchip on the workbench, next to the bookcase plans. I knew I'd find them here.

The directions look easy enough. 1, 2, 3,—logical, like Math. I can finish what Daddy Dean began, if I follow the directions carefully. Too bad Daddy Dean didn't leave me a diagram for being happy. Stop it, Wray Jean, I tell myself. That kind of attitude won't get this bookcase built.

I check the lumber supply. The shelving, cut and labelled, is stacked beneath a bundle of tall wooden dowels. Every year since I was five, I watched Daddy Dean stake Mama's tomato plants with dowels like these. As I move them out of the way, his instructions ring in my ears. *Feel this, smell this, taste this.*

I lift a board onto the sawhorses. The paper in the electric sander is worn smooth. I picture Daddy Dean in a cloud of sawdust, whistling his tinker's tune. I remember working this project with him, thinking we had all the time in the world.

I clip new paper into the sander. The familiar vibration travels up my arm when I switch it on. I'm all by myself. Yet I don't feel alone. My fingers fit comfortably into the worn places in the handle of the sander. As I run it over the board, the buzzing noise keeps me company. The smell of warm wood fills the workshop. This is my universe right now—this board and this sander and this back-and-forth motion. I catch myself smiling. I know why, too. I'm smiling because Daddy Dean is alive in this moment. If I had opened my eyes sooner, I would have found him in all his favorite places. Death has not captured my father. He is here, by my side. I feel him.

I feel Mama, too. I look up to find her studying me. The sander must have wakened her. I turn it off, waiting for her to say, "Come on out of there, Wray Jean. This isn't good for you."

Instead, she says, "Here you are down in the workshop at six o'clock in the morning. Bare feet. Pajamas. Sawdust on your nose. Do you know who you remind me of?"

I know who I've always reminded her of. She doesn't wait for my answer.

"You remind me of your father," she says. Her words travel through my veins, singing their way to my heart.

Mama is carrying two cups. She hands me one. I realize that this is not a woman who comes storming down the stairs just because she has been wakened out of a sound sleep. This is a woman who understands things without being told. Not all things, but some things. . . .

"Thank-you," I say, for more than the coffee.

I haven't used this mug for a long time. WRAY JEAN, it says. I'm not sure who that is. But someone who reminds my mother of my father can't be all bad. I stare at the letters spelling out my name. I notice how carefully they have been carved. As though the potter knew a time would come when I would take a closer look.

Mama clears her throat. She runs a finger through the layer of sawdust on my board. "Have you thought about the elections," she asks.

Have I? I'm not sure. "I could spend my whole life earning points," I say slowly. "But I think I've earned enough. I think I'm going to tell Mr. Sharp no."

No. It feels good to say the word out loud.

"Vice President is an honor I'll have to pass up," I announce.

Mama raises her mug, in a toast. "Good choice."

We'll see.

I'll have other opportunities. Besides, people with plans have to make sacrifices. Didn't I read that once? Well, I have plans all right. I'm going to work on this bookcase. I'm going to help Mama with her vegetable garden. This summer, when the cherry tomatoes ripen, I'm going to eat them warm off the vine. I'm going make room in my schedule for Rusty and Kayla and Poe.

I'm going to be happy, if I can.

I turn on the sander and press my palm into the shallow imprint of Daddy Dean's hand.

After this summer, I'll probably make some new plans.

But first, I'm going to write a letter to Hearthaven Home for the Disappointed. Maybe I should tell him I'm trying not to waste my time on things that don't matter so much. Or maybe I should just tell him this:

Dear Uncle Raymond,
I've seen him, too.

NOVELS FROM AVON ◆ FLARE

CLASS PICTURES	61408-1/$2.75 US/$3.50 Can

Marilyn Sachs

Pat, always the popular one, and shy, plump Lolly have been best friends since kindergarten, through thick and thin, supporting each other during crises. But everything changes when Lolly turns into a thin, pretty blonde and Pat finds herself playing second fiddle for the first time.

BABY SISTER	70358-1/$2.95 US/$3.50 Can

Marilyn Sachs

Her sister was everything Penny could never be, until Penny found something else.

THE GROUNDING OF GROUP 6	83386-7/$2.95 US/$3.50 Can

Julian Thompson

What do parents do when they realize that their sixteen-year old son or daughter is a loser and an embarrassment to the family? Five misfits find they've been set up to disappear at exclusive Coldbrook School, but aren't about to allow themselves to be permanentaly "grounded."

TAKING TERRI MUELLER	79004-1/$2.75 US/$3.50 Can

Norma Fox Mazer

Was it possible to be kidnapped by your own father? Terri's father has always told her that her mother died in a car crash—but now Terri has reason to suspect differently, and she struggles to find the truth on her own.

RECKLESS	83717-X/$2.95 US/$3.95 Can

Jeanette Mines

It was Jeannie Tanger's first day of high school when she met Sam Benson. Right from the beginning—when he nicknamed her JT—they were meant for each other. But right away there was trouble; family trouble; school trouble—could JT save Sam from himself?

ATTENTION TEENAGE WRITERS!
You can win a $2,500 book contract and have your novel published as the winner of the 1989 Avon Flare Young Adult Novel Competition!

Here are the submission requirements:

We will accept completed manuscripts from authors between the ages of thirteen and eighteen from January 1, 1989 through August 31, 1989 at the following address:
The Editors, Avon Flare Novel Competition
Avon Books, Room 818, 105 Madison Avenue
New York, New York 10016

Each manuscript should be approximately 125 to 200 pages, or about 30,000 to 50,000 words (based on 250 words per page).

All manuscripts must be typed, double-spaced, on a single side of the page only.

Along with your manuscript, please enclose a letter that includes a short description of your novel, your name, address, telephone number, and your age.

You are eligible to submit a manuscript if you will be no younger than thirteen and no older than eighteen years of age as of December 31, 1988. Enclose <u>a self-addressed, stamped envelope</u> for the return of your manuscript, and a <u>self-addressed stamped postcard</u> so that we can let you know we have received your submission.

PLEASE BE SURE TO RETAIN A COPY OF YOUR MANUSCRIPT. WE CANNOT BE RESPONSIBLE FOR MANUSCRIPTS.

<u>The Prize:</u> If you win this competition your novel will be published by Avon Flare for an advance of $2,500.00 against royalties. A parent or guardian's signature (consent) will be required on your publishing contract.

We reserve the right to use the winning author's name and photograph for advertising, promotion, and publicity.

If you wish to be notified of the winner, please enclose a self-addressed, stamped postcard for this purpose. Notification will also be made to major media.

<u>Waiting Time:</u> We will try to review your manuscript within three months. However, it is possible that we will hold your manuscript for as long as a year, or until the winner is announced.

VOID WHERE PROHIBITED BY LAW.